CURSE OF THE DRAGON HEIR

CURSE OF THE DRAGON HEIR

S. R. BREAKER

Zeta Indie Publishing

Contents

Best Laid

Trees shook when the slithery beast, half as tall as the forest ceiling, let out a fierce growl—cut short as two shimmery silver blades sheared the creature's spiky head clean off, the rest of its scaly body splattering in a shower of guts upon the verdant rainforest.

Soleia landed on the ground into a three-point stance with a heavy thud, her swords gripped in her white knuckles.

She blew the wisps of hair out of her eyes with a short puff, tossing a sideways look at the black thoroughbred waiting behind an overgrown myrtle tree. "That was even bigger than the last one, wasn't it, Boots?"

The horse snorted, giving his bridle a rattle. He jerked his head to beckon his master back.

"Cursed wraith forest indeed." Soleia shook her head as she straightened up with a grimace. She flicked the scarlet drippings from her blades before sheathing them in the double scabbard across her back with a swish.

"At this rate, we won't make it out of Ipera until sundown." She waded her way through the tall grass to retrieve the horse's reins off a high branch. "At least we know nobody else would be crazy enough to track us through here."

"And don't give me that look." She easily pulled herself back up on the saddle. "You know I had to get away from there. It's bad enough what today is." She curled her lips in distaste while adjusting her hold on the reins and kicked to trot off.

The first-born mages of the Priori Fae clan were special.

Aside from inheriting all the mystical powers of the Fae before them, they had great responsibilities. They were known and, therefore, always expected to do their duty. In particular, with the firstborns of the highest-ranking Fae family, her birthright was to eventually lead their people.

So, when the previous leaders of the Priori clan, wise and honorable as they were, had met their untimely deaths, the responsibility of leading fell to the first-born of the highest-ranking Fae mage family.

Caelina.

As the second-born of the family, Soleia couldn't have been more relieved.

And it had been good for the last twenty-one years.

That was until today.

Soleia clicked her tongue to instruct the horse to avoid a tangle of vines on the ground. "It's not like Caelina's ever needed me. She'll deal with it," she assured nobody in particular, or maybe herself. "She always sorts everything out. I mean, what more does the village need? Everyone already looks up to her because she's so perfect. She's never flunked out of tutelage or *allegedly* set fire to the supply shed." She paused with a mischievous grin. "Or ridden someone else's horse into a swamp."

The horse neighed as if in response.

Soleia chuckled and patted his mane. "I know, right? You made that jump right easy. Tobias' horse needs more gumption."

There was a reason Soleia felt more akin to her horse than to the other Priori.

She shared a lot of qualities with the thoroughbred. She liked to think she was serviceable, useful, if not impulsive at times. Being fearless, bordering on reckless—or perhaps smack dab right swimming in recklessness, often served her well enough to be adaptable under any circumstances.

On days like today though, she could have been better served with a semblance of a plan. Sneaking out of the village with Boots had been easy enough. But where was she even going to go?

Weighing her options, she sighed in deep thought.

There was talk of some towns across the impassable marshes, though nobody she knew had ever gone there and back again. She didn't even have a clue what lay beyond the mountain ranges of the east. But surely she should find a nice little village north of the Semi River. In hushed whispers, she had heard her sister talk to the elders of "human" settlements over that way, in protected realms where no magic thrived.

And perhaps if she didn't frighten these humans first off, she might offer her services as a hunter. She was a pretty good tracker.

She drew one sword to cut through the low-hanging vines, clearing a path in the thick forest. "Don't worry, boy. I bet nobody will even miss us anyway." A wave of despondence washed over her and she blew out another breath. "Especially once they find out that—"

Something rustled up ahead. Her eyes lit up and she immediately ducked low on her saddle, squinting to investigate the forward brush. Her heartbeat quickened in anticipation, in alert.

Was it more wraiths?

The tall grass shifted and waved before it finally parted to reveal an elderly woman emerging from the brush. She wore a worn woven cloak in the Priori colors and looked even more surprised to find Soleia a few feet away on her horse.

The woman seemed to collect herself quickly. As though in impatience, she moved the hand that wasn't holding onto her wooden staff to prop at her waist.

"Oma!" Soleia exclaimed.

Oermilla's wrinkled gray eyes narrowed even as her mouth had dropped open. "And what do you think you are doing here, child?"

Soleia's face paled at her grandmother's stern tone. "Nothing, Oma."

Oermilla tilted her head in suspicion. "Don't you Oma me right now," she chided, not really looking cross. "Everyone, as you well know, has been warned to keep away from this forest because of the dangerous wraith infestation."

Soleia sheathed her sword and dismounted to approach, but as she came closer, she noted Oermilla's hand just by her side. "What are those?"

About a foot each in length, a half dozen eel-like creatures wriggled in Oermilla's grasp where she had poised her arm, almost out of view.

The old woman held the squirming things out to show her. "Oh, these," she replied, offhand. "Baby wraiths. I caught them when I was taking a walk."

Soleia's eyebrows shot up. "You were taking a walk this close to the wraith forest?"

Oermilla gave her an even look. "Weren't you doing the same thing?"

She blinked, nearly in alarm. "Yes. I... I was just—I needed to think about some things."

Oermilla studied Soleia's expression as she set the baby wraiths on the ground and waved her hand over them briefly, making them stop wriggling. "Is something wrong, my child?"

Soleia pursed her lips. "No... I just..." She shifted on her feet. "I don't like our traditions. What kind of nonsense is it anyway that when mages in our family come of age, she should demonstrate her powers to the whole village?" She couldn't hide her grimace.

Oermilla gave her a meaningful, pointed look—one Soleia was familiar with, which meant she should have already known the answer to her question.

"It is a celebration of your skill. Not to mention an affirmation, a proof," Oermilla said. "It's to assure the people that our family, who have been entrusted with the leadership of the clan, will be capable of keeping the peace as we have for decades. It shows our people that they will be kept safe, that they will be protected, and increase confidence in our family."

Soleia kept making faces in insolence.

Oermilla gave her a stern look. "This is why I kept telling you, you should have been concentrating more on your casting training, instead of horsing around with Boots, and playing swords, and getting into fights with the village's warrior children."

Soleia rolled her eyes. "It's called sparring, Oma. I just...wanted to be able to protect myself with more than just silly magic."

"Silly?" Oermilla's eyes lit up. "My child, the magic of the Priori is a gift, and the magic you've inherited from my late sister is the rarest form of casting. Even your mother, bless her soul, didn't wield it."

Soleia had been told that Great-aunt Helene had once torn a hole through thin air, stepped through, and come back with an entire net's worth of fish fresh from the Semi Sea—a body of water clear across the Arcadian continent.

And apparently, one time when she was six, Soleia had, for several seconds, inexplicably popped out from and back into the schoolhouse, convincing her entire family that she had inherited this great, legendary skill.

"And there has not been a portal summoner in the clan for over fifty years," Oermilla raved on. "You understand how rare and special that is?"

As she was made to hear the tired, old platitudes all over again, Soleia wanted to kick herself. This was all her fault. She should have come clean years ago.

To be fair, Oermilla was right.

Soleia was indeed rare.

In fact, she was the first of their kind with virtually no casting magic whatsoever.

That being said, she would certainly fit into a "human" realm—if such a realm existed.

That show of "power" when she was six had been a complete fluke. Since then, Soleia could do little more than the warrior Fae, cast little spells—make things glow, barely anything to be useful.

For years, Soleia had done her best to make sure everyone's impression of her was wholly preserved.

In the meantime, what else could she do? She needed to learn to take care of herself another way. As often as she could, she undertook to train with the village's warrior families' children instead. Taking to avoid magical chores at the village in favor of joining the hunting parties where she at least could be useful.

Except for tonight, she was expected to perform at the ceremony in front of everyone to show just exactly how magical she really was, just like every member of her family had before her when they had come of age.

Soleia would rather face the cursed wraith forest.

"You should be getting back. The sun is past its peak in the sky and you'll need time to prepare." Oermilla moved to take her elbow.

Soleia jerked her arm back from Oermilla's grasp, but it was too late.

Oermilla gasped as if she'd been struck. "You were running away."

Soleia stepped back. *Dammit.* She should have been more

careful around her grandmother's heightened senses of perception, and with Soleia's already frazzled mind, she wasn't strong enough to keep her surface emotions buried sufficiently.

Her tone reprimanding, Oermilla went on. "And have you been killing the wraiths? Has your grandmother taught you nothing? You know you can put the small ones to sleep if you just cast a spell..."

Soleia looked away and bit her lip. Yes, yes, of course, she knew all that. She knew exactly *what* to do but...

Her wary gaze flicked back over to meet Oermilla's, worried she had already gleaned what Soleia had been trying to hide for nearly fifteen years.

"Soleia... You don't..." Oermilla was already shaking her head in astonishment.

A wave of nausea hit Soleia, and she whirled around to run away, momentarily forgetting about her horse. Her heart was pounding in her chest. *She knows! She knows!* Her throat tightened in panic and dismay, but she willed her feet to keep moving, her grandmother's calls sounding farther and farther away.

"Soleia, no! You're headed too far into the—"

Her foot squelched in a mud puddle as she tried to avoid deeper ones.

The Priori had all also been told that the bigger wraiths thrived deeper in the forest. Soleia had roughly mapped her earlier escape route to skirt around the forest's edges, but right then, she just needed to get away.

Get away from her grandmother.

Get away from her life.

Get away from the truth.

The moment she remembered she had left Boots behind, she glanced back to check.

Soleia tripped, "Oh shit—" and fell face first in the mud.

She hadn't noticed another clump of vines on the ground near a clearing beneath a large cedar tree. Now they were tangled over her feet.

After a moment and a groan, she pushed up on her elbows, looking up, but she stopped short, spotting strange yellow symbols carved into the dirt just before her.

It seemed to exist apart from the wet ground, even as it imbued the same with an odd golden glow.

Soleia tilted her head to one side in curiosity. She stood back up only to gasp in shock at the sight of a man pinned high against the tree trunk. The cedar's gnarled roots had grown wrapped around his limbs and across his torso.

He wore a textured armor suit that seemed like it should gleam if not for the layer of dirt and soot caked on, his face hidden beneath his mud-coated long hair as his head hung.

She would have thought he was merely unconscious if not for the fact that what fastened him up against the tree was a long silver sword with a jeweled hilt shoved right through his chest.

Though for a dead person in such a remote location, he seemed rather well-preserved, as there was no evidence of rot or decay.

There was obviously some form of strong magic at work in this place.

She blinked, stepping back. "What the actual f—?"

Oermilla's rushed arrival swirled the leaves on the ground. "My child—," she began, breathlessly.

Soleia met her gaze with an incredulous glare. "What is this, Oma? Who is that?" She pointed to the body against the tree.

"It's nothing," Oermilla dismissed. "You must forget you ever saw this and ask no questions. Now let's run along before—" She tried to veer her away with another grasp on her elbow, but Soleia shrugged her off again.

She studied the telling look on her grandmother's face. Oermilla was definitely hiding something. Giving her a pointed look, she challenged, "Oh my god, Oma, what were you really doing here in this forest?"

Oermilla pursed her lips. She would have been well-versed in Soleia's stubbornness and knew she had to tell her something. Taking a deep breath, she resigned. "The wraiths serve to protect this sacred place, to keep our people away from this cursed demon."

"Right..." Soleia nodded. "But there's always been wraiths in this forest—" Her eyes lit up as something clicked in her mind.

The baby wraiths.

She gave Oermilla an incredulous glare. "Oma, did you—*have* you been planting the wraiths in the forest all these years to keep our people away from this...whoever this is?" She waved in disbelief toward the cedar tree.

Oermilla turned her gaze away, but her silence was answer enough.

Soleia's jaw dropped, but before she could voice the

overflowing turbulence of questions in her mind, the ground beneath her shook. *What the—?* Her eyes widened.

The dirt before them stirred and before Soleia could make out what was going on, a long, black creature slithered out from under the ground.

"Soleia!" Oermilla stood and put both hands up to cast the wraith away, but when its tail emerged from the dirt, it whipped at her, tossing her frail figure into the thick brush, rendered unconscious.

"Oma!" Soleia cried out.

She intended to run toward the brush to see if her grandmother was all right, but the next thing she heard was the hissing of the giant wraith. It darted toward her and wrapped around her neck.

"Aagh!" Soleia yelped as the grimy beast wound around her body. She tried to grasp at the creature's girth to yank it off, but it was constricting tight. She couldn't even wail in pain as she choked, her arms flailing around in desperation.

She cast Oermilla's knocked-out form amongst the brush a wide-eyed, panicked look.

Help me!

Soleia squeezed her eyes shut, trying to breathe.

Somebody help me!

2

Cursed

The wraith rose on its long, sturdy tail with Soleia constricted within its folds. Her feet no longer touched the ground.

Dammit— Soleia clenched her teeth in determination. She wasn't about to die here today. Not by a stupid wraith's doing. She grunted out loud to push her arm out of the creature's vise-like grip to slide down her side, reaching for the dagger by her hip.

After an eternity of breathless counts, her fingers finally gripped the hilt, and in the next split second, and with a muffled cry of effort, she lashed the blade against the bit of the beast around her neck. The dagger severed into the beast's flesh, loosening its grip enough to drop Soleia to the ground.

The wraith hissed out loud in pain and recoiled. Soleia grasped it by a fold, yanking with all her might to throw the wraith straight across the clearing.

Gasping, Soleia watched the beast's landing disturbing the tall grass and bush. She knew it would be back.

"Bravo."

A deep voice from behind startled Soleia and her gaze snapped up toward the sound.

His eyes were open.

The cursed demon pinned against the tree was awake.

Soleia's eyes popped wide in shock. "What the hell—?"

But the demon simply went on with a dry, mocking drawl as though there wasn't even a giant sword shoved right through his chest. "Seriously, Helene, why are you wasting so much time with a dumb wraith? Just snap your fingers and banish it into oblivion."

Helene...?

Soleia could only stare up at him.

He didn't like it. "What's the matter?" he sneered. "Can't handle a little worm monster anymore?"

Soleia swallowed, her voice little more than a mumble in confusion. "I am not Helene."

"You look pretty pathetic just standing there gawking."

She clenched her jaw again as his words struck a nerve.

"Come on! Do it like you did me. Or are you finally feeling your age? Your weary bones catching up to you, eh, Helene?"

"I am *not* Helene!" Soleia repeated, her tone bordering on annoyance as she straightened up.

The demon stopped short, sniffed, and likely catching a slightly different scent, his eyebrows quirked for a split second to study her face a bit more closely.

Soleia knew she had inherited her Great-aunt's silvery-blue

eyes and all the women in their family had the same brown tresses but when the demon's eyes narrowed again, she could tell he had realized his mistake.

A small moan dragged Soleia's attention away and she spun to rush toward the brush to find her grandmother. "Oma..." She braced her arm under Oermilla's shoulders to support her.

Oermilla pushed herself up on her elbows, her gaze zeroing in on the cursed demon in the tree. Her eyes widened bigger than Soleia had ever seen them. "He-he's awake..." she mumbled as she struggled to get up. "But how?"

Soleia's gaze snapped toward the other side of the clearing where a loud rustling indicated that the dreaded, giant wraith was coming back. "Never mind, Oma. The wraith is coming back."

Worry must have been obvious in her tone that the demon huffed airily upon overhearing. "I can take care of that ugly beast in two seconds. Not like you, a pathetic weakling. Obviously."

Weakling.

The word set her blood boiling.

Soleia shot a glare at him. "You shut up!"

He growled, his eyes blazing. "Release me and I'll kill it for you. I eat monsters like that for breakfast."

Oermilla weighed in with a loud hiss. "Shut up, demon." She regarded Soleia as she stood back up, hunting around for her staff. "Soleia, don't listen to him. Let's just get out of here."

Soleia turned back toward the ominous rustling sound of the wraith in the bush coming closer. Her heart pounded in her chest.

She'd killed nearly a dozen wraiths today already. What was one more? Especially now that she wasn't caught off guard.

"Soleia, what are you thinking?" Oermilla asked in knowing dread.

Amused, the demon watched Soleia's stance as she got in position to fight. "The girl wants to die, lady. Except she's obviously too weak to defeat that creature. I'm the only one strong enough around here to waste that monster so now how's about you release me?"

Soleia sneered, reaching over her shoulders to withdraw both her swords. Stupid demon. She'll show him how weak she was.

Quick as a flash, the giant wraith sprang out from the bushes again, darting toward Soleia and Oermilla. "Oma, stay back!" Soleia yelled out as she pounced onto the creature, slashing her swords in a fury, rebounding away, and leaping back to strike the monster at several points along its length before she jumped as high as she could to slice through its side.

The forbidding creature spasmed erratically, hissing and curling its long body, and with a defensive snap of its tail, it flicked Soleia away while its head snapped at her blades.

"Oof—!" Soleia hurtled toward the muddy ground. She blinked back her bearings in time to see her swords get tossed all the way into the brush on the other side of the clearing. "My swords!"

The demon laughed.

The wraith reared back with a loud hiss and was making to swoop in for another strike.

Soleia scrambled backward, her palms slipping in the mud,

her eyes darting around in frustration before she glimpsed the glint in the sword stuck through the demon's chest and she shot up to reach for it.

Oma's eyes widened as she cried out, "Soleia, no!"

But Soleia clasped her fingers around the hilt and pulled, frowning for a moment in surprise at the extra effort it was taking. She grunted and pulled harder, a small smile curving her lips as she finally felt it budge—only to have the weapon completely dissolve in her hand, into nothing.

"What the—?"

"Soleia!" Oma cried out.

The demon bent his head to hide his spreading grin before a beam of light burst out from its body, sending a shockwave of energy throughout the forest, throwing Soleia and Oermilla to the ground once more.

The demon roared his triumphant laughter.

The next thing Soleia saw was the demon speeding up the length of the monster's leathery body. As though fuelled by his hate, the demon bared his sharp claws and began his frenzied slashing, slitting the wraith neatly in half, right from head to tail, tearing straight through the monster. Its ferocious growls mingled with his.

It only took a few seconds then the wraith's body stilled for a moment before exploding across the forest in another shower of bloody guts.

The demon landed with a hard thud on one knee back on the grass, his arm held out to one side for balance as he let out a breath.

Then he lifted his sharp eyes to meet Soleia's.

She gasped and was barely able to react when he launched

himself into the air again, his claws already bared to strike her down.

There was a loud clank as Oermilla wove into the way with her staff, blocking the demon's attack and he rebounded away.

"Oma! What—? I-Is he trying to kill us?" Soleia panted.

Oma's expression was grave. "You've released the demon. Now it won't stop until we are all destroyed." She stretched her arm out to keep Soleia behind her. "Stay back, Soleia. This creature is more dangerous than a hundred wraiths combined."

The demon appeared up the path with a sly smile on his lips but he didn't rush at them this time. Instead, he chuckled as he examined his bloody claws.

"You're looking old, Oermilla," the demon mused. "How long has it been—fifty years from the looks of you?

Before Soleia could wonder how the demon could possibly know her grandmother's name or what his statement implied, Oermilla growled at him, her expression more fierce than Soleia had ever seen.

"She's not Helene," she rasped. "Helene is dead. You leave my granddaughter alone."

His eyes narrowed for a moment. "Do you think that matters to me?" he demanded. "I was stuck on this tree for decades because of her *and* you! And just because the stupid girl released me doesn't make up for what you've done. It doesn't settle our score for a second."

Soleia tilted her head in curiosity. "What is he talking about?"

"Soleia, run. Run back to the village," Oermilla instructed.

She puffed up her chest in indignation. "I'm not leaving

you, Oma. Let me get my swords back and I'll finish off this pompous jerk."

The demon laughed. "She has no idea who she's dealing with, does she? Maybe it's time to show her."

Oermilla's eyes widened. "No—" She stepped back and put both hands in front of her to begin casting.

But the demon hissed and pounced on her, knocking her back to the ground before he rebounded against a tree trunk and launched himself toward Soleia next.

"Shit—" Soleia scrambled away, running toward the grass across the clearing. She had to find her damn swords! She felt frustratingly and ridiculously helpless without them. She tore back the weeds in search of her weapons while the demon followed in hot pursuit. She cried out, mostly in aggravation as she kept running, over and under fallen logs, around vines, in an attempt to confuse him.

Oermilla's voice rang out in the din, almost inaudible in the distance. "Force him back toward the blessed realm!"

The demon grinned as he chased her. "You're pretty nimble for a foolish girl."

Soleia growled, yelling back, "You're pretty vengeful for someone whose life I just saved!"

His eyes blazed. "Saved? You think you saved my life?"

"Oh, I'm sorry," she panted, vaulting over a mud puddle. "You would have preferred to stay trapped on the tree."

Soleia's eyes flickered to the ground. The demon didn't seem to notice that she had led him back to the tree. But just as she was going to grin in triumph, somehow he appeared in front of her. She screeched to a stop, her scream trapped in her throat.

Soleia pivoted quickly to try another offensive run at him but instead, he caught her by the neck and lifted her off the ground.

He laughed even as she choked and struggled to get out of his grasp. "This is for the last fifty years," he declared as his fingers lengthened, his claws sharpened, and his skin began to blister and turn as his body made for his transformation. The wind swirled around the clearing, whipping the leaves and branches about as the demon's energy pulsed, his hazy form growing larger.

"Soleia!" Oermilla's frantic voice rang out from still way across the clearing.

Soleia desperately tried to turn her head to meet her grandmother's gaze. Out of the corner of her eye, she noted Oermilla stop short amidst the weeds and raise both hands just as Soleia's eyesight blurred. *NO!* She screamed in her head.

An ephemeral glow formed around the demon. As though a sudden, sharp pain gouged into his chest, he doubled over, losing hold of Soleia. He fell to the ground on his knees, his hands flying up, pressing against the sides of his aching head, and with another loud growl, he collapsed on the ground.

* * *

3

Bonds

"Someone smells of horse."

Soleia turned dull eyes toward her sister across the dais of the otherwise empty assembly room. "For god's sake, I'll wash up later, okay?"

In complete contrast, Caelina was rosy clean in her stately satin gown, a hand-stitched, embroidered cloak around her shoulders bearing the Priori seal, her hair impeccably tidy in a braid trimmed with colorful beads coiled up around her head. She waved away someone at the door before another wave of her hand slid the panel shut.

Oermilla paused for a moment by the entrance to ensure their privacy. It was in no one's best interest that the village be alerted as to who, or what was under the woven blanket the two women had dragged in here earlier.

She took a turn around the assembly room, her movements causing the large windows to shift and shrink until they were but narrow slats high up near the ceiling, solely to let the light in while discouraging curious onlookers, and the bustle outside as the villagers prepared for the evening's festivities muted to their ears.

The evening's demonstration was traditionally accompanied by a festival, music, dancing, and food—a Priori thanksgiving celebration that had scarcely changed in centuries.

Normally, Soleia and Caelina would be decorating the theatron, livening up the roads with banners and lanterns, making sure the cooks knew where the food was meant to be laid out, and testing out the new delicacies.

Today, there were more pressing matters at hand.

But Soleia was only half-listening to her sister's reprimand when sharp claws scraped the wooden floor. In a heap in the corner, the unconscious demon had finally stirred.

"Oh, he's awake."

With a jerk, the demon jumped to his feet. After a split-second's stocktake of his predicament and spotting the three women at the dais across the room, the glower on his face darkened and he immediately rushed toward the group, his eyes blazing in fury as he bared his claws once more.

He'd pounced into the air before Soleia cast him a momentary glance and rolled her eyes. "NO."

An invisible force struck the demon and he came crashing down. "Ow!" he yelped.

Blinded by fury, he didn't seem to notice the string of beads glowing around his neck as he scrambled up in aggravation before roaring and trying to jump them again.

Soleia's tone was even as she said the word again, "NO."

The demon's collision with the wooden floor was

accompanied by a loud and furious, "OW—dammit!" Only then did he glimpse the beads around his neck. "What the hell is this?" But he tried yet a third time to attack them—in vain, crashing face first and wailing in agony.

"Don't bother, demon," Oma advised. "With the ancient binding spell I've cast, those beads now hold your spirit, and even with all your power, you will be unable to remove it."

The demon growled and yanked and pulled on the necklace in vehement desperation—to no avail.

Having established that the demon was no longer an immediate threat, Caelina heaved a huge sigh. "Now then..." she went on with an authoritative, disappointed glare back at Soleia who wasn't even looking at her. "Have you even been listening to me?"

Soleia grimaced in distaste, not meeting her sister's gaze. Instead, she watched the demon struggle with the beads as he rolled around, tumbling in frustration and effort before crying out in unhappy rage.

Caelina was definitely not happy either. No doubt, this was the last thing she needed. Especially today. She cast Soleia another begrudging look. "Can we talk about what the hell you were doing in the cursed wraith forest, to begin with?"

Soleia's jaw dropped in indignation. "How about we skip to the part where Oma was in the cursed wraith forest, planting blasted baby wraiths?"

Caelina pursed her lips.

Oma shrugged as she approached the pair of them. "It's too late now. She needs to know."

Soleia's eyes widened. "You knew about this?"

"I was informed when I ascended as leader of our clan.

Guarding this secret used to be our parent's duty before it fell to me."

"And now to you as well," Oermilla put in, giving Soleia a short nod.

Caelina gave Oermilla a suffering look. "Which brings me to my next question—Oma, for god's sake, why did you bind the demon to my sister?"

Her face wrinkling further, Oermilla scrunched up her shoulders. "The great tree spirit had gone," she pointed out. "You know as well as I that once that sacred bond is broken, you cannot restore it. My spirit would have been too weak to hold him. It would not have been safe. Soleia's was the only other spirit there."

Caelina could only groan. Oermilla was right. Highly inconvenient, but right.

Soleia was still watching the demon with a grimace. "Are you sure we're all going to be safe with him walking around freely like that?"

The demon had relatively settled down, lying on his side on the floor facing away from them, still snarling as his fingers repeatedly yanked hard on the enchanted string of beads around his neck. But he seemed in deep thought as if reassessing his options.

Oermilla nodded. "The cursed beads will prevent him from harming anyone. Only the one to whom he is bound can take them off or indeed break this curse. Only you can give the word, child, and you must mean it strongly."

Soleia made a retching sound, sagging her arms in complaint. "Why can't I just kill him?"

Caelina sniffed. "This is not your pet uquix all over again,

Soleia. After begging our parents to get you one, you can't leave it at the village bounds in the hopes that someone else adopts it simply because you've grown tired of the responsibility."

"You're the one who almost set fire to my uquix!" Soleia cried out in protest. "Mother and Father wouldn't even believe me! He was never the same after that."

Caelina stuck her tongue out at her.

"Girls!" Oermilla snapped.

"Ugghh..." Soleia groaned long and loud. "Fine." Her eyes imploring, Soleia looked up at her grandmother. "This isn't forever though, is it, Oma?"

Oermilla gave her a steady look before gesturing toward the ruined patches on the tatami floor and mending them. "It will only be until we find another way to bind the demon to make sure we are all safe," she assured. "We have been charged with making sure this creature is not let loose upon this world. I've seen first-hand the destruction he is capable of. He will destroy everything at his first opportunity."

Caelina clicked her tongue, her eyes cast to one side. "But the fact that you released this monster into our midst is not going to win our family any goodwill. The warrior's elders are already skeptical of my leadership. They believe I favor our mages. They question me at every turn." A shadow crossed her face as she dropped her gaze. "Mother and Father always made sure to keep the peace. But now, without them...we are weaker."

"We are weaker regardless." Oermilla sighed as she gazed out the high window. "The magic of the land is not what it used to be. We are the last of the Fae. It is important for us to endure. We *need* to endure, to preserve our traditions. We must reassure our people that we *will* survive."

If Soleia's heart wasn't heavy enough before it certainly was now.

Caelina would never have recklessly tried to fight a giant wraith and accidentally release a dangerous demon into their midst.

She cast another glance over at the sulking figure across the room. "What is he, really?" Her eyes narrowed in curiosity. "And what he was doing stuck to that tree in the first place?"

Caelina waved her question away. "We can discuss that tomorrow. Can we just—please get through one family event without it being a complete disaster? Please?" she asked, her gaze on Soleia expectant. "Now go and get washed up and ready for tonight. You need to be presentable, reassuring."

Caelina didn't say it but Soleia heard a third adjective. *Powerful.* She cringed, her pulse racing in apprehension again. Was it fair? To have this weight of expectation thrust upon her? She mumbled in derision. "Sure, sit on your throne and plan your little parties. Everything comes so easy for you."

"Easy?" Caelina mocked, her teeth clenched. "You think leading our people is easy? When our parents passed..." Her tone faltered. "I had other plans too, Soleia. You think you're the only one who's got the right to complain?"

Soleia wanted to kick herself again, immediately regretting her words. If there was anybody else in the world who understood the pain of losing their parents, it was her sister.

Caelina's voice trembled just a slight. "I have worked hard to create a stable environment for the Priori. They are our people. Our duty is to them." The expression on her face softened in exhaustion. "Now do as you're told for the first time in your life."

Soleia dropped her gaze in shame, which quickly transformed to dread at Oermilla's next statement.

"You and I still need to have a little talk, Soleia."

Soleia bit her lip. She had almost forgotten that Oma had had a little insight into the reason she had been running away. Something she was absolutely not eager to rehash. At least not until after a bath.

"By the way," Caelina piped up, her nose wrinkling toward the demon. "That one also needs a wash."

4

Demon

Her stupid plan had stupidly failed.

Soleia should have been halfway across Arcadia, enjoying her freedom, in places where nobody even knew who she was, or what she was supposed to be able to do or be responsible for, and not have all these huge expectations.

Instead, she was back in her same village, and in charge of babysitting a stupid demon. To top it all off, she was going to be humiliated in front of her entire people when she would have to "demonstrate" her stupid powers for the sole purpose of reassuring everyone.

Also, she really did now smell of horse.

She grimaced, picking out wraith entrails from her braid, only looking up when a stocky blond young man and a girl with sharp, dark eyes appeared strolling down the road. She gave them a careless wave. "Tobias. Anelis."

"I heard a rumor we're keeping a demon in the village,"

Tobias remarked, approaching Soleia to lean against the hitching post by the washing shed. "Where exactly have you been, you sly loner?" He nudged her shoulder. "I should have known when you didn't turn up at the pastry cart this morning. What were you thinking trying to run away? You were going to leave us behind and not even say goodbye?"

Anelis narrowed her eyes. "Everyone knows you can't keep secrets, Tobias."

Tobias pouted. "Still. So much for friendship."

"So what sort of mess have you gotten yourself into again?" Anelis went on with a self-satisfied smirk. "My father said no good could possibly come from that massive shockwave earlier. Everyone felt it. I should have guessed you had something to do with it."

Soleia rolled her eyes. "Stick your nose in someone else's business, Anelis." If Tobias was the closest thing Soleia had to a friend, Anelis was more of a rival.

"I'm pretty sure the safety of the entire village is everyone's business," she remarked, her nose high in the air.

"So where is it?" Tobias pressed, darting his eyes around. "Is it out here? Shouldn't it be in a cage or a mile-deep hole somewhere? Isn't it dangerous?"

Soleia jerked her thumb back towards the small wooden cabin down the lane behind her. "Not right now, he isn't."

Suddenly intrigued, Anelis' eyebrows shot up her forehead. "He? It's a he?"

Tobias snickered. "Just because you lost Juric to Soleia, have your standards fallen so low as to consider a demon instead?"

Anelis shoved him away. "Shut up, Tobias. And I didn't

lose to Soleia," she added. "It's not like I put my name up for it when the elders were deciding on these matches. Besides, I never liked Juric anyway." She folded her arms across her chest to make her point, unconvincing as it was.

Soleia let out a small sigh. "If it makes you feel any better, Anelis, I never liked Juric either."

Tobias tilted his head to give her an even look. "Soleia, Juric is from a good warrior family. Your union has already been agreed upon. It would strengthen both bloodlines. Your sister has chosen well for you in your parents' stead. They would have chosen the same."

"They certainly chose well for *Caelina*," Anelis quipped, gesturing with her hand. "Stellan is super hot."

"Oh yes, the warrior genes in that family, wow. I mean if his brother was still around, you two might not even have a chance. I would have…" Tobias trailed off from his tangent before clearing his throat. "The point is, Soleia, you need to take your place among our people, accept your responsibilities."

Soleia knew Tobias wouldn't stop his sermon unless she acquiesced so she blew out another breath in feigned resignation. "I suppose you're right. You're always right."

"Speaking of super hot brothers-in-law," Anelis whispered, her gaze having drifted off over Soleia's shoulder.

Soleia turned to see Stellan walking over.

Tall, lean, his loose robes concealed his strong warrior's build. He had a bundle of clothes in his arms and a deep frown on his famously, uncommonly handsome face, the displeasure on it aimed squarely at Soleia and he wasted no time to let her know.

"What were you thinking bringing that dangerous demon

into the village? Haven't you caused enough trouble for this family?"

Soleia sneered at him even as he walked past the three of them to dump the pile of fabric on a shelf inside the washing shed. "Then ask the great Oermilla why the hell she bound the stupid demon to me! This is not fun for me, you know? Why do I have to be the one who has to make sure he doesn't hurt anyone? I have better things to do."

"If he harms Caelina, I'm going to kill you."

Tobias and Anelis didn't even get a word in edgewise before Stellan cast them all a glare and sauntered away.

Soleia scoffed as she watched him go. *He can try*, she thought smugly. She was just as good as any of their warriors. She would gladly take on Stellan if only to see how fast she could make him fall on his back.

When he and Caelina had been united three years ago, the village had been overjoyed. Stellan was a strong warrior. Caelina was a strong mage. It was another perfect match blessed by the elders. Despite that, Soleia was grateful that Stellan seemed to make her sister happy.

In the last few weeks, however, Stellan had progressively become a cranky stick in the mud. He was already a bit of a jerk before. Now he was nearly intolerable.

Tobias clicked his tongue. "Arrogant or not, I still love to watch him walk away."

Something else had stolen Anelis' attention entirely. "Oh-oh my god, is that him?" she practically rasped. "The demon?"

Soleia glanced over toward the washing shed, only to jerk her gaze away.

Having finished his bath, the demon was getting dressed, and apparently, he didn't care if anyone saw his naked bottom through the slats in the shed window.

But her friends were staring, their jaws having dropped.

Tobias mumbled, "Holy mother..."

Soleia bit her lip, and after a moment, figuring there was no harm, she turned back to join the two watching the demon shrug Stellan's clothes on.

They looked even better on him too as the loose-fitting tunic complimented his broad shoulders. The demon certainly cleaned up nicely. His long silver-white hair was no longer caked with mud and it was neatly half-tied back.

Soleia furrowed her eyebrows noting the scars on his back, his arms, his hands—scars like he'd been through hell. He was certainly a warrior too.

The way he efficiently fastened the buttons on his cloak with his strong fingers made something in her stomach stir.

Having had the occasional encounter with the men in their clan, they were, in Soleia's experience, mostly unremarkable. All the Fae mages were meek and all the warrior Fae were oafs. Still, they provided enough entertainment for a spell.

On the other hand, she could imagine this demon was neither meek nor oafish.

Tobias couldn't help a small squeal of excitement and the demon's gaze snapped up to catch them spying.

His gold-red eyes pierced right through Soleia and even with the knowledge that he could harm no one because of Oermilla's spell, a chill still ran up her spine.

He wasn't dangerous. But he wasn't safe either.

Surely if he was in full control of his power, she, Anelis, and Tobias would likely already have been ripped to shreds— just like the wraith.

Soleia indulged a curious moment of wonder at how different he might be had he the opportunity to use all his powers. Except she would likely not live to see it, as she was certain, his first act upon being released from the curse would be to end her.

* * *

Despite their curiosity, Tobias and Anelis could not be persuaded to stay and help keep an eye on the demon.

Humid air pungent with fragrant herbs wafted against Soleia's face as she stepped into the washing shed, in time to see the demon wrestling with the necklace in another attempt to yank it off.

His gaze turned sharp when he looked up to meet hers but she cracked a slight grin. He probably couldn't believe he was at the mercy of a "weak" little Fae woman.

The demon had tried to escape twice more before the guards could lead him to the washing shed but it was nothing the binding word from Soleia couldn't easily handle as every false move he'd made had earned him, at the very least, a face full of gravel.

"Do you enjoy this?" he prompted, his voice low and deep as of a growl. "Watching me suffer? You're worse than Helene."

"Hey, I didn't choose this either, Curse Boy." She feigned a hurt look as she walked past him to peer behind the door where a couple of attendants were already refreshing the steamy bath.

"If you're going to address me, I suggest you use my given name."

"Why would I do anything you suggest?"

He merely growled again. Given how evil he was, he was probably unused to anyone speaking to him that way.

Perhaps it was lucky Soleia was still unaware of his true nature.

Perhaps if she knew what he really was, she would be very afraid.

Three female warriors entered the hut and took to stand at their positions at three corners.

The demon sniffed. "What are they doing here?"

Soleia bid the attendants a wave before she stepped past the door and closed it behind her. "They're here to make sure you don't make any trouble while I get all this wraith and forest stink off me," she spoke through the door. "The last thing I want is you attacking my people while I'm washing my hair. Now stay put and shut up unless you want to smack your face on the floor again."

She couldn't help a sigh as the fresh warm water in the tub soothed her aching muscles. Then, gritting her teeth in instant annoyance, she rubbed the dirt off her fingers, under her nails, and smeared in her tangled hair. She was used to getting into scrapes and getting all muddy but today's was a whopper.

Rustling from behind the door caught her attention and she glimpsed a large shadow looming in the bottom gap just as the shadow of the female warrior guarding the door stepped away.

She narrowed her eyes in suspicion. No screams though. She hoped the demon hadn't frightened away the three warrior females she'd asked to keep guard. Though it was more likely they were simply too afraid of him and wanted to steer as far clear as possible.

But just in case...

"You ladies yell out if he makes even the smallest wrong move, alright?" she called out.

Three 'yes's reassured Soleia and she relaxed in the bath, not that she could take her time as usual. Dangerous demon on the loose, responsibilities, and whatnot.

There was another soft growl and Soleia could just guess he was still fiddling with the string of beads around his neck in dismay.

"You realize what you're doing is pointless, right?" she couldn't help but quip.

Instead of answering, he started, "I gather from your village there's some kind of festivity tonight. That's what you were trying to escape, running into the forest, wasn't it?" His question was muffled through the wooden wall panel but she heard him.

Soleia let out an exasperated sigh. "Well, that doesn't matter anymore, does it? Because here I am, back to fulfill my duties, like a responsible little mage." She flicked some water out of the tub in impatience. "If my sister wants me humiliated in front of the entire clan, they're welcome to it. I'd better not catch them at the end of my blade. Seriously, I will gut anyone who laughs."

She thought she heard a deep chuckle from the other side of the door.

"Maybe we can make a deal and convince your grandmother to bind me to something else."

Soleia cringed. "I'm really not in the mood to ask any favors from her at the moment. So I suggest you accept your lot in life. That's what I'm going to do." She sighed heavily again as she finished up. "There's no other way for me. I will be humiliated among my people, an outcast like always."

"Come on, you know we've both got a raw deal here. You don't want to be bound to me any more than I want to be bound to you."

She recognized his tone—personable, friendly. He was obviously trying to get her sympathy, trying to get in her head, find out what he could offer her, and lure her into a false sense of security before slitting her throat.

It wasn't going to work. If she had to face humiliation in front of the entire Priori tonight, then he was going to have to put up with his spirit being bound for all his sins.

She drawled in response, "And yet here we are. Me with all the responsibility. And you with all the evil."

When Soleia stepped out, she had already put fresh clothes on, two layers of cotton and moleskin tights above her boots. Her cloak hung over her arm for the moment and her hair was still wet and in a disarray about her shoulders.

The demon was right outside the door. His forehead creased as if in displeasure at the sight of her but he took her in for another long minute, looking her up and down in wonder. "How old are you?"

"None of your business."

"Are you mated yet?" His voice was gruff but deeply rich.

She shot him a glare. "That's none of your business."

The three warrior females exchanged looks.

Oh, great, Soleia thought in derision. Now they were probably going to start rumors about her and the demon. Just what she needed right now. "Thank you for your help." She dismissed the females with a wave before hanging up her cloak and turning back to fix her hair.

His scrutiny was unnerving her and also making her stomach do somersaults.

Stupid stomach. What the hell was wrong with her anyway? He was a cursed, dangerous demon that would destroy them all with one swish of his claws if given half the chance.

She cleared her throat, hurrying to finish grooming so she could exit the cramped indoor space, feeling a bit more cramped than before.

"Let me free."

Her eyebrows rose in incredulity at his words. "So you can kill me and everyone I know?"

He visibly swallowed hard. "I won't."

Soleia gave him a dull look. "Right."

His forehead creased in aggravation. "You don't even know who I am! How do you know it's justified to hold me against my will? How do you know you're not in the wrong here?"

"Look, the only wrong thing I did today was take too long at that dumb wraith forest. I should have ridden faster, fought harder. I should have just left some of the smaller wraiths alone. If I could have just put them to sleep, I could've—" She stopped short, blowing out a frustrated breath.

His eyes narrowed. "I thought you handled yourself quite well."

She gave him a deadpan look. "I know exactly what you're doing. You're trying to ply me with compliments so that I'll feel sorry for you or something and maybe release you from Oma's binding spell. But I'm not that dumb, Curse Boy."

He blinked like he didn't expect her to figure that out and he merely huffed in displeasure and looked away.

Soleia smirked. She was quite enjoying having so much power over him. "What kind of a dumb demon gets trapped on a tree anyway? And then to finally get free of the tree, only to get trapped by a necklace! Is this only the second curse that's been put on you? Or have there been more?"

That set him off.

He growled again, grabbing her by the shoulders and pinning her back against the wall.

She almost rolled her eyes at his futile intimidation efforts. Did he forget one word from her would send him doubling over? She met his gaze, undaunted. "You didn't scare me before. You definitely don't now."

He roared, leaning close to her face. He was clearly displeased, infuriated. "Mark my words," he rasped. "This spell *will* break. And when that time comes, I guarantee you, you *will* be scared. And then you will die."

"Right, whatever. But until then, Curse Boy, your life belongs to me." Soleia gave him a shove to push away but he pressed harder.

He was focused on her mouth. "Dathon," he growled. "My name is Dathon."

He spoke near her face. His freshly-showered scent was almost hypnotizing, overwhelming. Her chest heaved against his in her struggle to breathe and he must have noted her heart pounding. His incensed gaze seared into her.

Soleia blinked her senses back into focus and threw up her hands. "Fine!" And at her concession, he let her shrug him off. "Whatever."

5

Big Deal

Caelina wasn't kidding when she said that night was a big deal.

Standing at the theatron, Soleia had never seen the village looking so festive. Lanterns, paper chimes, and multi-colored banners hung across the lamp posts which lined the streets where Fae warriors and mages alike all dressed in their best were promenading. Ipera was a glistening valley haven in the clear, cool night.

It made her feel even more sick to her stomach, even more nerve-wracked about her demonstration.

Soleia had tried again and again earlier today to cast something, even a tiny illusion—anything, but the most she could muster as per usual were little sparks of light that fizzled out in mere moments.

Plus it was hard to find alone time to practice, what with the dumb demon tailing her everywhere. Or rather, that she had to keep him in check to make sure he wasn't doing anything untoward.

Caelina had said to lock the demon up in a cage for the rest of the night, but Soleia was in the firm belief that no cage they could construct would likely be strong enough to contain him.

He was quite a tricky demon, already almost sneaking past a handful of warrior guards again this evening if not for Soleia's sharp eyesight and four more consecutive NOs. Honestly, she could have kept going with it all night.

Although, that seemed to have wised the demon up somewhat. He was sulking in the shadows by the elevated stage, right where Soleia had instructed him to stay until the celebration was concluded.

Perhaps he had decided to finally give her a break, she mused before correcting quickly. *Right.* Like he would be so amenable to giving her a break. With her luck, the demon would probably start a commotion right when she was called to showcase her magic. It might serve as the perfect distraction but she certainly didn't want anyone in the village to get hurt because of her carelessness.

Ugh. Yet again, she wanted to kick herself for continually claiming through the years that she had more powers than she actually did.

Truth be told, she was hoping her magic would eventually manifest. It was the only reason she hadn't gone through with running away much sooner, despite all the years of planning to do so. She had heard of late bloomers in their clan before. It was only unfortunate that even as she had come of age, her powers still had yet to show. That was, if they were there at all.

She glanced past the crowd, to the path into the thick forest again. It was dark now but still not too late to escape. She would simply need to distract her sister and grandmother. And once she had escaped, she would just kill that demon they had so thoughtlessly bound to her. She couldn't very well have him tagging along, could she?

Her neck warmed at the recollection of when he'd blown up at her in the washing shed. The look in his eyes, the roughness of his voice, they seemed to hold a heavy promise.

Of death?

Possibly.

Soleia looked up when Juric and his father approached her and her family at the theatron.

Tarik, Juric's father, was an esteemed warrior elder. Soleia knew Caelina was hoping the union would smooth over current relations with the Priori warriors.

The pair of them walked up to Oermilla, in her comfortable chair sitting to one side of the stage, to show respect before the father approached Caelina and Stellan for pleasantries and Juric came to her.

"Soleia." The young man took her hand in greeting.

To give Tobias and Anelis' taste some credit, Juric was certainly good-looking, fair-haired, and built. He was a well-respected warrior in the clan as well.

Caelina must have been right that he was the best match for her. And with his being a strong warrior and her being of the strongest mage family, it would very much make for a terribly pleasant and stable atmosphere for the clan and all that nice and safe reassurance everyone was chattering on about.

Except Juric would certainly reject her once he found out that she had no powers. His family would never accept the match.

Perhaps it *was* better to show everyone and have done with it after all. Soleia had had enough of keeping secrets. Maybe once everyone found out how worthless she actually was, they would finally leave her alone. And then she could run away.

She cast another wistful glance toward the path leading to the dark forest.

"Soleia," Caelina snapped, jerking her head toward Juric in a reminder for her to pay attention.

A big smile on his wrinkled face, Tarik lifted his cup toward the lot of them. "We look forward to many grand occasions such as this. A toast to the future generations of our people." He tilted his head in a nod to Oermilla who was beaming in response before turning to meet Caelina and Stellan's gaze again. "And may I say congratulations as you prepare to welcome an addition to this new generation quite soon?"

Caelina's cheeks colored, her soft smile but a hint of her immense happiness.

Stellan merely let out a chuckle, his handsome face glowing.

Soleia nearly choked. Her narrowed gaze dropped to her sister's belly upon which Stellan's protective hand rested and her eyes widened.

Oh my god.

Even as she was blindsided by the news, a rush of elation

shot through her. Fleeting, as she was next filled with a horrible realization.

If she had actually run away today, she would never even have known, would never have met her niece or nephew.

Regret tore at her heart, but at the same time, she wanted to escape even more.

Caelina being with child only highlighted another thing Soleia was nowhere near a point in her life to be capable of achieving. Yet another shortcoming.

Her throat tightened in anxiety. She couldn't breathe.

Completely forgetting about the dangerous demon she was meant to be keeping an eye on, Soleia turned from the theatron and fled.

6

Weapons and Lies

Soleia ran to the same place she always did. Her favorite sanctuary. The smell of the stalls had never once bothered her and the soft whinnies of the horses always set her spirits at ease. In the quiet, away from all the people, she could usually think more clearly.

Usually.

Groaning, she squeezed her eyes shut.

Pregnant! Caelina was pregnant!

No wonder Stellan was being so touchy lately.

Soleia didn't quite know what to do with the news. It was good news, she supposed. A new addition to the family. A continuation of their glorious bloodline! Oermilla was probably overjoyed. Their family would endure. Soleia was going to be an aunt. She was going to be a terrible aunt. She was a fraud.

It was all just so confusing.

Lost in her thoughts, she frowned as she brushed Boots' hair. "What are we going to do, boy?" she whispered.

The stable door slammed open, startling Soleia. She gasped, whirling around.

"What are you doing?" The demon sauntered in. He looked around the otherwise empty stables, looked at the horse, then back at her in complete annoyance and puzzlement. "Are you running away again?" he demanded. "Look, the pain from these beads is unbearable. If you're going to run away, I need to know so that I can adjust my own schemes. And I'm not too keen to test the range on your binding word."

She hissed at him. "I wasn't running away. I just needed to think."

He seemed to accept that response, his posture relaxing. Then his expression changed. "You left your mate," he mocked with a sly curve on his mouth.

Soleia groaned.

"That's who he was, wasn't he? That boy speaking to you. Your mate."

"Ugh, I hate that word. He's not my mate. Not yet anyway. Besides, he just happens to be the only eligible male from the strongest warrior family in the clan." She stopped short, taken aback. "Also, blasting hell—!" She threw her hands up in irritation at her own loose lips. "This is none of your business!"

The demon grinned. "I could tell you weren't happy with your intended. I have to say your displeasure pleased me. I would wish you never to be happy."

She gave him a suffering look but didn't indulge him with a further response and went back to grooming Boots.

But the demon seemed at a loss. He didn't want to stay

but he couldn't leave. He cast an aimless glance around, another perpetual frown on his face. He blew out a deep breath. "Look, if you wanted to escape, why don't you just conjure a giant cloud of fog to cover the village? Nobody would even notice if you slipped away. I hear it's one of the easiest bits of air magic, even a weakling like you won't break a sweat."

She shot him a wary look.

His eyes lit up. "Oh! Is that why you couldn't deal with the wraith in the forest? You don't have any magic at all."

"Of course I have magic!" she barked. "And if anyone overhears your yapping, I will end you. Don't give me a reason to disobey my sister any further because honestly, right now, the smallest, tiniest reason to do so will serve me *so* well."

She groaned again, dropping the brush since, in her fury, she might be hurting Boots. Overwhelmed with a wave of desolation, she dropped her gaze as well. At a complete and total loss.

The demon tilted his head as if to gauge her mood. "Look," he began evenly. "I understand as much as feeling trapped even whilst being out in the wide open. Just release me and we can both escape this place—" He stopped short to amend, "And by that I mean, separately of course." He tugged at the string around his neck. "Take this off."

Soleia gave him a resolved look. "I'm not going to help you. You're a demon."

As if in offense, he stiffened, sticking his chin up. "I'm also a man. Your grandmother has been misled." He gave her a meaningful look. "I'm actually a prince from a faraway land and I've been trapped here in this realm by mistake. I never meant to harm anyone. My cause has always been to protect the innocent. And I've dedicated my entire life to—to—"

His voice shook for a moment before he gave in to his shout of laughter. "I'm sorry. I can't even go through with that speech. You're right." He nodded, the menacing expression returning to his face. "I will kill you and every other idiot in this village. Then I'll go on my merry way and kill every other arrogant Fae I come across."

Clearly not amused, Soleia gave him a deadpan look.

But the demon went on, "Oh, hell," moving to wipe tears from the corner of his eyes. "I made myself laugh."

"Congratulations."

"Was I about to convince you at all?" His eyebrows lifted up.

"Not in the least." She turned to put away some of the horse tack.

Grinning wide, he shook his head. "I can't wait to watch your blood flow once I've gutted you."

Soleia gave him a sideway glance. "Charming."

The demon must have had acutely-honed senses, he cocked his head first.

After a few moments, the faint rumbling reached Soleia's ears as well and she frowned. "I hear it too. It's coming from outside the village...but it's getting closer."

Boots neighed and stirred.

"Sshh..." She stroked his mane to calm him down before moving toward the stable window facing the road. She craned her neck to attempt to see what the growing commotion was being caused by.

A distinct scream punctuated the appearance of what from afar looked like a dark tower emerging from behind the theatron right at the end of the main road but except for noting a few villagers running away, Soleia couldn't see what—

The demon came up beside her. "What the hell is going on?"

She squinted. It wasn't a dark tower. It was—

Then her jaw dropped and she stepped back. "I-It's-"

It was the biggest wraith she'd ever seen.

This creature was easily twice as big as the one from earlier. She was so on edge that she jumped even at the familiar voice from the doorway.

"Soleia, there you are."

She blew out a relieved breath and came up to take her grandmother's arm. "Oma, it's just you. What's happening?"

Oermilla pursed her lips, her tone grave, her gaze flickering toward the demon by the window. "The demon's curse used to keep the wraiths contained in the forest. They fed on his energy. It kept them pacified. But now that he is out and the great tree spirit is gone, the wraiths are venturing further to seek out mystical energy."

Soleia cast him a pointed look in accusation. "So this is all your fault?"

But the demon just shrugged. He likely couldn't care less about the wraiths.

Oermilla put her hand on Soleia's shoulder. "Stay here, my child. If you are indeed powerless, you'll be better off to hide."

Even the demon noted the indignation rise in Soleia's chest.

Powerless. Weakling.

She hated being called those things.

"But—"

Oermilla had already left to rally the mages and warriors to defend the village.

Frustrated, Soleia raced to follow her out the doorway only to be thrown back inside by an energy shockwave. She slammed against the stall gates before sliding to the floor, momentarily winded.

Moaning as she regained her bearings, she struggled to straighten up. "What the hell was that?"

The demon peered out the window. "All hell is breaking loose out there," he observed, quite unconcerned, casually inspecting his claws.

Soleia's gaze darted left and right, clenching her fists to get ready regardless. She figured Caelina must have also already dispatched the warriors but they didn't have the experience or the scale to fight off such a monster. She recalled herself being far from effective with her swords to even hurt a creature of half such a size.

In the next second, she was flooded with an even worse fear.

Caelina! Caelina would be fighting the wraith. She could get hurt. Her baby could get hurt. Soleia needed to help protect the baby. She needed to help preserve their future.

Snapping herself out of her frozen terror, she turned to get Boots ready, adjusting his reins and straps. When she glanced out the window again, her eyes widened in dread once more. "Oh god, the theatron is on fire." She reached back to draw a sword. "I have to help them."

The demon who was simply watching the goings-on as if it were entertainment shot her a strange look. "I thought you wanted to escape this place? Who cares what happens to it?"

Soleia swallowed hard. His question echoed in her mind.

How selfish it all sounded. And yet, it was all true. Only earlier today, she would have abandoned her entire village, her only family. After a few frenzied breaths, she stuck her face up to meet his gaze in resolution, willing her chin not to tremble. "My sister is pregnant."

The demon's eyes narrowed. The frantic, overwhelming desperation must have been clear in her face, in her voice, in her flurry.

He glanced away for a second. "Give me your sword."

Hurriedly leading Boots toward the door, she shot him an incredulous look. "Like hell I'll trust you with a weapon."

He tugged on the horse's reins to stop her. "My claws will be less than useless with a wraith this size. I'm going to need a blade. You have an extra one anyway."

"It's not an *extra* one. I happen to need two."

"A strong fighter would only need one," he asserted.

She shot him an annoyed look. "It's a style. Shut up!"

He tugged on the reins again. "Give me one of those swords."

"No way."

He gritted his teeth, leaning closer to her. "I can't hurt you anyway, remember?"

"But you might hurt my family, my friends." She stuck her stubborn chin up to him again.

He rolled his eyes. "Give me a weapon." His hand moved to grasp the hilt already in her hand, his firm gaze boring into hers. "Or your whole town will be destroyed, *including* your family and friends."

Soleia's gasp caught in her throat as he stared her down, and almost involuntarily, her grip loosened on the hilt.

His eyes cleared but he kept his gaze pinned on her. He took the sword without another word. And just when Soleia thought he might turn the blade right at her neck, he whirled around and charged outside.

She blinked, snapping to attention, hopped up on Boots, and followed suit.

"You go for the middle. I'll go up top," he yelled back at her before disappearing into the darkness.

For a split second, Soleia's stomach turned over in dread. Was the demon gone? Did she let him escape? With her favorite weapon? Did he use this unique opportunity to dash away?

She shook her head. If he did, it was too late. That didn't matter now. She had to help her family.

Closer to the theatron, the chaos and disarray were arresting. Banners and flags were torn. Toppled lanterns burned small fires lining the road. An assembly house had been decimated, scattered kindling on the ground.

Charred smoke laced the air, tickling Soleia's nose. Her eyes blurred as she rode past several bodies lying on the ground. Were they alive? Were they dead? She gripped the reins tighter and rode faster toward the screaming.

The giant wraith was thrashing around the village center, its tail whipping around, smashing through more huts and trees. The growl it let out was more of a screech that reverberated into the night.

Several of the village's warriors were leaping at it from the tops of houses, shooting arrows and spears at its wide girth. A small group had shot a rope tied to a harpoon to topple the wraith over or to secure it.

A bright glow caught her eye. Oermilla and Caelina along

with Tobias, Anelis, and a group of other mages were casting from beneath the creature.

Soleia dodged falling debris as she rode Boots closer to their group.

"Oma! Caelina! I can help!"

Caelina's eyes lit up when she appeared. Not letting go of the magic cast from her fingers, "Soleia! Can you summon a portal big enough to send the wraith away?" was her first question.

Soleia's heart stopped. *Shit.* She steadied her chin. "What else can I do?"

Caelina looked confused but Oermilla cut in. "Soleia, see if you can gouge out the monster's eye! Its power is focused there. Once it's removed, we can attempt to subdue the beast."

Wide-eyed in alarm, almost not blinking, Soleia nodded. She darted a look toward Tobias and Anelis but both of their faces were crumpled in concentration as they focused their casting on the creature. She warily met her sister's puzzled gaze for another brief moment before signaling her horse to ride away. "*Hya!*"

Soleia's mouth was dry, her heart pounding in her chest. *Weak. Powerless.* She tried to shake it off but she was too distracted; she didn't see the tail of the wretched creature whip toward her.

"Soleia!" a deep, loud voice called out the warning.

She gasped in fright, catching sight of the tail at the last minute, and jerked Boots away just in time. She lost her balance and fell off the horse. But it was a better result than having been tossed away by the monster's tail.

Boots neighed, rearing back, his hooves in the air before he rode off a few feet down the road to circle back for her.

Once she stopped rolling on the ground, Soleia scrambled to crouch low behind some bushes. Out of the corner of her eye, she glimpsed a dark shadow leap from out of nowhere. The shadow roared as it ran up the length of the wraith wielding a blade that glinted when it caught the moonlight.

Soleia couldn't stop her jaw from dropping.

He didn't leave.

And he really was bloody impressive.

Her eyes lit up in alert. "Get its eye!" she yelled as loud as she could.

He must have heard her. She watched as the demon nearly ran vertically up its length before roaring to jump high up above the creature's spiky head and slashing and gouging at its eyes like mad.

Just then, the wraith snapped its razor-sharp teeth and the demon tumbled headlong to the ground.

Soleia only heard a muted yell but was in no doubt that he had been badly hurt. *Oh no.* She sprinted toward the clearing and found the demon in a heap, cloak torn, unconscious, among the tall grasses.

She bent down to retrieve her sword and was about to spin around and leave, but she stopped first, hesitating. She cast a glance back down at the demon on the ground before darting a glance up at the wraith. It was moving away, moving deeper into the village.

After a moment, she groaned in resignation before bending down beside the demon to inspect his injury. Red coated her hands as blood gushed from his side. "Oh-oh—oh god..."

A streak of blinding light emanated from the village. Oermilla and the mages were working more of their magic.

She gritted her teeth and sheathed the sword again, whistling for her horse. When Boots arrived, she struggled to hoist the bulky demon up behind the saddle, hopped on, and rode for the village again. "*Hya!*"

She rode alongside the huge monster, trying to keep out of its destructive wake as it slithered along. She could hear more screams coming from the village.

Her heart pounded even harder in her chest as she kicked Boots to go faster, the demon's heavy form thumping behind her.

All of a sudden, the creature's midsection wove into their path, completely blocking the road. The now-blind creature was thrashing around. Oermilla and the mages were probably making progress to weaken it.

Except it was still in her way.

"You stupid monster," she muttered bitterly.

Soleia drew her swords again and raced toward the length of the creature to slash her way straight through its flesh.

The stupid monster had ruined everything. If there hadn't been any wraiths today at all, she would have been able to escape the village in the first instance. She would have been freed of all this, freed of her responsibilities, freed from her humiliation.

Soleia just wanted to be free.

Why couldn't she just goddamned be free?

"Aaahhh!" Soleia screamed out loud as she raced toward the beast—just as a faint glimmer appearing right in her path burst into a large spiral of bright, blinding light, and even as she tried to pull on Boots' reins, it was no use as they hurtled straight through.

* * *

7

Late

Soleia could barely breathe with the stifling heat. She pushed up on her hands, her fingers digging into the coarse sand beneath her.

Her vision was hazy but she spotted Boots across the way as the horse straightened up with a whinny. Still unconscious, the demon was lying by a shallow puddle on the rocky ground near the horse.

The intense afternoon sun beat down against the towering jagged rock formations casting a temporary haven of shade beneath it along one side of the terrain. On the other, dried brown smatterings of vegetation popped up randomly across the miles and miles of sand and dunes.

What the hell happened?

Her throat gritty, Soleia still tried to swallow as she assessed her location.

The giant wraith monster was no longer in sight. They were obviously no longer in Ipera, *nowhere near* the forest village.

Soleia's heart pounded in her chest as she recalled the bright spiraling light they had charged through. She had only fragments of descriptions from stories from when she was a child of what one looked like when Helene summoned them. But it couldn't have been. Could it?

A portal...?

Ridiculous.

Impossible.

She shook it off, groaning as she straightened up to limp over to Boots.

The black horse neighed, adjusting its footing on the uneven ground as Soleia took the reins. "Where the hell are we, boy?" she whispered, scratching under his neck.

"What did you just do to us, witch?"

Soleia's gaze snapped to meet the demon's as he squinted up at her, the sun in his eyes. Unfortunately, his battered, drooping form, not to mention his indignant tone indicated that he had no idea what had happened either, that much was certain.

Her stomach churned in apprehension and knowing dread at the nagging conclusion she didn't want to accept and she didn't respond. Instead, she clicked her tongue, maneuvering the horse back so she could bend down to collect water before washing her bloodied hands, a little more forcefully than she needed to.

The demon seemed about to pass out again but he tilted his head to regard her with a look. "Are you a portal summoner?"

Soleia blinked up at him, wide-eyed at his confident guess.

One corner of his mouth turned up. "Helene was a portal summoner," he recalled. "You're the exact same witch. But a lot less pretty."

She had almost forgotten that the demon somehow knew her Great-aunt. She merely shifted her glare onto him. "At least it looks like you've finally gotten exactly what you deserve."

He coughed at her remark. Though, he was likely more annoyed at the numbing pain in his side more than anything.

She went on. "You're lucky I know you're harmless."

"Oh, come on." He wheezed and coughed again. "*You're* lucky I'm in pain. Otherwise, I would end you right now. If you've got any smarts at all in that pathetic brain of yours, you'd run away while you have a chance. Run far, far away."

She furrowed her eyebrows as she gave him a once-over, considering his words, but she only bent to collect her strewn swords and sheathed them back before taking the horse's reins. "Don't move. I'll come right back."

He sneered between coughs. "If you do, I'll kill you and everyone you know, if only for causing me so much trouble."

Without another word, Soleia hopped up onto the saddle, "*Hya!*" and rode away.

Was she tempted to leave the cursed demon out in the desert to his certain death?

No doubt whatsoever.

But aside from the debt of gratitude she begrudgingly now had to him, his company likely wouldn't hurt in this unfamiliar wilderness—if only to use as bait to distract any predatory beasts to give her time to escape.

Besides, she needed to at least survey the lay of the land before figuring out what to do next and the injured demon needed to stay put.

Her chest still tight with apprehension, Soleia gripped the reins tighter in her hands.

She should have been elated. She should have been over-joyed. She had finally summoned a portal. But why now? Why couldn't she have helped her family dispatch the wraith before any of this even happened?

She muffled a frustrated groan. There was 'better late than never' and then there was *this*.

She didn't even know how she had done it. Fae mages were supposed to control their magic, not the other way around. It was almost worse than not having any magic at all.

And now she was stuck in the middle of nowhere.

Lost.

Then again neither Caelina nor her friends would be surprised.

So true to form, Soleia, she scolded herself but immediately shook it off. Gritting her teeth in determination, she kicked Boots to ride faster.

Soleia had only ventured to the top of a ridge and right back down but the demon must really not have expected her to come back at all. Boots' neighing visibly jerked him awake from his half-conscious stupor.

The demon was collapsed onto his side on the rocky ground, having to make an effort to turn his head in time to glimpse Soleia riding back and his eyes narrowed.

The horse screeched to a stop a few feet away from him

and she dismounted before she unhooked a bag of water from her pack and took a swig, her eyes cast across the desert.

"The hell are you doing back here?" the demon croaked out.

Soleia turned to give him an even gaze. "We're miles away from any settlements. I could barely see any structures from the ridge. You're going to have to stay put until we sort out that gash in your side."

The demon's eyebrows shot up in surprise.

Soleia stroked the horse's mane. "What do you say, Boots? Shall we go when the sun sets so it's cooler or would it be safer to go on in the daylight?"

"How's a horse supposed to respond to that?"

She ignored him.

"Only an idiot would journey through an unknown terrain in the dark," he declared.

"Only an idiot would journey through the desert in the heat of the day," she retorted, not looking at him.

He grunted in mid-question, "Why don't you just portal us away like you did before?"

"I can't."

"Why not?"

She threw up her hands, yelling, "I can't, alright?"

"Alright, jeez! Settle down." He coughed again as he tried to sit up. "And you said you had magic."

"None of your business!"

He almost snickered, except he lurched over with another groan first. "Oh, hell—it stings."

Soleia blew out an exasperated breath. "I need to have a look at your wound. Take off your shirt."

That made him pause. His eyes glinted and his mouth curved into a sly grin. "Oh, you'd like that, wouldn't you? I saw you and your friends watching me earlie—" He broke off, clutching at his side.

Not responding to his baiting, Soleia rummaged in her satchel. She pulled out a couple of bottles, a small jar, and a bit of binding fabric. She didn't have a needle. She wasn't a healer. She was going to have to make do.

"Why did you come back?"

She squared her shoulders, her chin tilting up. "You helped save my village. That means you get two seconds of mercy."

He cast her a suspicious look. "Are you sure that's all? I've been told by many consorts that I'm quite good to look at."

"For an evil demon," she replied deadpan. "I came back because I believe in paying debts. You saved my village, my family, and you saved my life. In return, I offer to save yours."

His eyes measured her and she studied them right back. She could almost already tell exactly what he was scheming.

"If you're thinking you're going to seduce me so that I'll set you free, you can forget about it. Now unless you'd rather die here and now, take off your damn shirt."

The caught-off-guard look in his eyes gave away that she had guessed his plan exactly—again, he looked away, huffing in displeasure. "You are so annoying." He groaned as he tugged on the hem of his shirt and pulled it off.

She shifted closer to examine his side and grimaced. She wouldn't have been surprised if she found his internal organs spilling to the ground. She poured some water over his wound to wash away the dirt and dregs.

He clenched his fists at his sides.

She furrowed her eyebrows, reaching for the smallest brown bottle, and doused his wound with it.

He growled as it stung and jerked forward almost hitting her head with his. "*Goddammit*—is that alcohol?"

She didn't respond, concentrating on binding his wound.

He hissed again as it smarted. "Stop that!"

"Hold still!"

He roared again, grabbing her shoulder almost involuntarily as he dropped his head, squeezing his eyes shut as he heaved.

Frowning, Soleia watched him get a hold of himself.

Right then, he didn't seem any more dangerous than any Fae male she had ever met. And she didn't doubt for a moment that many consorts found him pleasant to look at. His fully human appearance gave no hint of his real nature.

She half-expected a vile creature such as he was to have unappealing characteristics, perhaps bumpy skin, some manner of deformity, an overall repulsive essence.

There was absolutely none of that. His perfect form could have been sculpted by the gods.

Be careful. She closed her eyes for a moment to focus again on what he really was.

He was a demon, more dangerous than a hundred wraiths. He was going to destroy them all, that's what Oermilla had said. She had to remember that.

She removed his hand from her shoulder so she could shrug off her cloak to lay it over him for cover.

Besides, if she had to look at that bare chest for long,

despite her convictions, there was no telling where else her thoughts would stray.

His eyes narrowed. He glanced down at the cloak before looking up to meet her gaze again. He seemed surprised but there was something else in his eyes.

Soleia glared at him. "Why are you looking at me like that?" she snapped. "I suppose it must have been over fifty years since any woman touched you, huh?" She pushed quickly away to straighten up, dusting herself off. "For your information, I've also been told by many a warrior from my village that I'm quite good to look at."

He huffed, looking away. "Slim pickings."

She gritted her teeth, tamping down her ire and looking away herself. "Oma says you can't kill him," she chanted to herself. "Oma says you can't kill him."

He let out a half-groan, half-chuckle as he shifted on the ground, propping himself against a rock. He blew out a heavy breath in fatigue before prompting, "So you *are* a portal summoner."

"No."

"Then how the hell did we get here?" he challenged. "I think you've brought us clear across the continent. I recognize those mountains. We're in the desert Outlands."

She followed his gaze to the mountain range at the far end of the sandy, hazy landscape. "So we are."

Soleia had never been this far this side of Arcadia before either. She wanted to marvel at the stunning landscape, bask in the triumph of finally discovering for herself what was beyond the eastern mountain ranges. But her wonder was overridden with apprehension.

How in the hell were they going to get back to Ipera?

Frustrated that she didn't know the answer to her own question, she chugged a mouthful of water from her satchel and without another comment, tossed the bag toward the demon.

He had to jerk to catch it and groaned again as his wound twitched but instead of complaining, he downed a big gulp.

"You were trying to run away before," he noted. "I guess you finally succeeded."

Soleia shook her head. "Now I need to go back."

"What?"

"And you have to help me."

He almost sputtered out his latest mouthful. "Me help you?" He was going to laugh but he stopped short at her next words.

"Do you want this curse removed or not?" She gave him a pointed look, already satisfied that the offer was enticing enough for him. "You seem to be familiar with this area. If you help me get back to Ipera, I'll make an official request to Oma to remove your curse."

His gold-red eyes almost glowed but his face soured. "And how are you sure she's going to listen to you?"

"If you don't help me, I really will just kill you right now, no matter what my grandmother says. I'm not traveling with dead weight either."

He snarled, glancing away.

Soleia gave him an expectant look, one that ought to brook no argument. "So do we have a deal?"

He scoffed. "Do I have a choice?"

"Yes."

"Is death the other choice?"

"Pretty much."

Dripping bitterness, he muttered his response. "You've got yourself a deal."

She clasped the hand he offered out to her at their bargain. "Then it's a deal, Curse Boy."

He gripped her wrist. "Dathon."

Her eyes snapped up to his and she tried to jerk her hand away, but he held her gaze and wouldn't let go of her arm. He was a lot stronger than the severity of his injury should have left him. His eyebrows lifted in his firm prompt.

She blew out an aggravated, resigned breath, and swallowed hard before speaking, "Dathon."

A ghost of a triumphant smile crossed his face.

Soleia snatched her hand back, giving his airy smirk another glare before settling cross-legged on the ground across from him. "We'll need to stay put until sundown," she relayed matter-of-factly, glancing up at the sky. "Then we can make our way back to Ipera..." A shadow crossed her face as she trailed off.

His gaze had not left her. "What?"

"Nothing."

"Nothing?"

She dropped her eyes and only spoke after a moment. "What if they're all dead?"

His forehead creased but he gave her a steady look. "They're not. We blinded the creature. From what I saw, your family is strong. They should already have the creature handled."

"What if the other wraiths come?"

"I'm sure they'll have thought of a way to keep the creatures out by now." He couldn't help a dry scoff. "Maybe they found another innocent soul to bind to the cursed tree to attract the wraiths."

She gave him a suffering look. "You think that's funny, huh?"

"Yes."

She shook her head. "What am I even thinking? You're an evil demon. Of course, you laugh at others' suffering and have no feelings. You probably don't even know what it's like to have a family, do you?"

Momentarily taken aback, the demon growled in response but only turned his head away.

8

Enemies and Allies

On the brink of dozing, Soleia jerked up in her seat. *Shit.* Did she fall asleep?

Wide-eyed, she glanced up to meet the demon's gaze.

Plain boredom was etched on his face, and he simply averted his eyes. He was still sitting across from her, her cloak draped over him.

Her pulse raced. He could have slit her throat while she slept. He could have stolen her horse and ridden away, leaving her stranded in the darkening desert. He could have knocked her unconscious, tied her up, and sold her to the nearest trading post. He could've—

With a soft groan, Dathon shifted in his seat.

Soleia sat up. "Are you still bleeding?"

He merely grimaced. "I heal fast. Also, I've had worse."

Clearing her throat, she smoothed back her hair. With a hiss, she rubbed her hands over her arms in the cold. Without the sun to warm the desert, the night air was brisk, particularly right by the mountain ridge as caused by the downdraft.

Noticing her movement, Dathon's forehead creased.

"Here."

Soleia gawked at the cloak he was handing back to her.

He fidgeted in his seat again and turned his head away, his lips curled in derision as though regretting what he'd just done. "We're almost out of water," he mumbled.

She grabbed the satchel he tossed in her lap and chugged the last mouthful.

As Soleia put her cloak back on, she couldn't help her gaze straying toward the sculpted contours of his chest where the moonlight cast interesting shadows, but she dragged her attention toward the wound in his side. Her eyebrows lifted in astonishment. "You do heal fast."

"I told you," he quipped but then caught her staring.

She snapped her eyes up to his, self-conscious, and unable to stand the cocky smirk that appeared on his features, she threw his shirt at his face. "Put your shirt back on."

Dathon's grin widened even as he complied. "If you're interested in a little tumble, I don't mind playing with my prey a little before I kill it."

She gave him a suffering look, reminding herself yet again that he was a dangerous demon. "I prefer to kill my prey before I eat it."

At the notion of a meal, his stomach rumbled and he frowned down at it. "Oh."

In spite of herself, Soleia couldn't help a chuckle. Having skipped all the festival food, she was hungry too. It was lucky

Boots had been packed for her failed runaway mission. She dug in her pack for a bag of dried fruit and seeds and tossed it at him. "Don't finish it all."

He drawled. "What a feast."

Making a face, she pushed up to stand again. "So sorry, your highness, but that's all we have." She approached Boots to start packing up again. "If we had more time, I could have scrounged up some sand eels, made a fire—"

"Ugh. I hate eels." He curled his lips in distaste, his words muffled as he chewed. "Also if you don't have any magic, how are you going to make a fire?"

Soleia rolled her eyes. "The old-fashioned way, of course. I'm pretty good at it." Then she smiled in self-satisfaction. "Caelina could never properly master fire casting."

"Is that your sister? The one who's pregnant?"

Her heart thumped in her chest, in worry, in dread. But she took a deep breath and shook it off. Halfway across the world, there was nothing she could do for Caelina at the moment. Ignoring his question, she cast him a glance. "If you're done snacking, we should get ready to go. The closest settlement is still about ten miles east. We need to get supplies, some water."

Dathon jumped to straighten up, all limber, and apparently back to full health. He passed her back the bag of food and moved to take Boots' reins.

"What are you doing?" She pushed him aside. "It's my horse."

He blinked at her. "Are you intending for me to walk ten miles?"

She tugged on the reins. "It's my horse."

"There's only one horse," he pointed out. "We can share or take turns."

"It's *my* horse," she repeated evenly, folding her arms across her chest.

"I'm injured, you evil woman!" He shot her an incredulous look. "Besides, if I let a pathetic Fae weakling like you lead, we'll probably get lost in two minutes. Or more likely," he amended, "with your luck, we'll probably end up in quicksand or a sinkhole somewhere, or die of exposure—"

Soleia let out an aggravated yell as he droned on and on. "Ugh!" She resisted the urge to tear her hair out. "Oh my god —why can't I just kill you? Dammit, Oma!"

He guffawed. "Let's see who kills whom first."

She gave him a skeptical look. "You could have killed me when I fell asleep earlier. Why didn't you when you had the chance? You're looking all recovered already anyway."

He folded his own arms across his chest. "I believe in paying back debts too," he huffed. "But I won't be so generous next time. Besides, it would have been no challenge at all. I could finish you with my bare hands in the blink of an eye if not for this." He yanked on the string of beads around his neck.

Soleia looked amused. "Are you saying I can't take you without that spell on?"

"I'm saying the only reason you are still breathing is *because* of this spell."

Her jaw nearly dropped in offense. "Try me, Curse Boy."

His eyes narrowed. "I told you, my name is Dathon."

"Your name is whatever I deem it unless you beat me," Soleia challenged.

He lunged at her without warning.

"Agh!" She staggered backward before shooting him a dirty look. "What the hell? I wasn't ready!"

Dathon straightened up in his stance, shifting his weight from one foot to the other, beckoning her. "Come on then."

She hissed in response before pouncing at him.

He ducked to avoid her swinging punch, weaving left and right to avoid her next two strikes. "Gods, you're fast!" He grinned, tumbling on the ground, and rolling twice more in an attempt to catch her off-guard from behind.

Soleia yelped as he swept her legs out from under her. She fell to the ground, sand and dust fluffing up around her. She clenched her fists, growling in displeasure before jumping right back to her feet and lunging at him.

Dathon bobbed and she missed again. Except for—

He heard the rip from his sleeve as she had got him with a sneakily-pulled dagger. His eyes blazed as he glanced up. "Who said you could use weapons?"

"I can use weapons," Soleia declared.

He scoffed. "I don't need weapons to beat you." He bared his claws, striking them together with a swish as he squared off again, knees half-bent, shoulders tight.

But Soleia thought she caught a glimpse of a smirk on his mouth. His eyes danced as she lunged again, brushing close enough against him to hear him breathing. His scent was all around her even as she dodged his next strikes.

"You're pretty good, Princess."

"Don't call me Princess," she balked at the word.

"Don't call me Curse Boy," he retorted as he pounced past her, tugging on her braid.

"Hey!"

His grin was all kinds of mischievous and doing funny things to her pulse.

Bad demon. Bad demon. If he kept distracting her, she would surely lose. Irritated, she shook it off to focus and finally caught him with a quick sweep and he fell on his back with a thump and a cloud of dust.

"Ha!" She propped her knee on his chest, pushing down ever so slightly.

Heaving, Dathon's eyes dropped to the shiny dagger, cold under his chin before he looked up at her. Gasping herself, she met his gaze. She didn't say anything but the surprise on his face was victory enough.

"Alright." Dathon slowly moved to sit up, putting his hands up in defeat. "You win," he claimed. "You can put your little dagger away."

Soleia let out a breath, dropping her guard a moment too early and before she could straighten up, Dathon pounced to tackle her.

Her eyes popped out but it was too late to defend herself.

Dathon's pre-emptive, triumphant laughter was cut short by her cry.

"NO!"

He crashed face first to the ground from her uttering the curse's binding word. "Ow—what—!"

Jumping in indignation, he spat out sand and pebbles

from his face as he wiped his sleeve across his mouth. "That's cheating! That's not the rule."

She gave him a bemused look. "What rule? I guess I win."

He roared in displeasure. "You fight dirty."

"I fight well," she corrected.

Dathon met her blasé expression in annoyance and utter disbelief.

Soleia was still heaving but the look in his eyes was another unspoken challenge.

He wanted to kill her. But more than that, it was as though he wanted to wipe the smug look off her face, wanted to conquer the wild spirit in her eyes, wanted to contain it, or perhaps drown in it...

He grabbed her arm, pulling her close, his voice low and husky. "Seriously, how about a little tumble? I'll even put off killing you until tomorrow."

Soleia willed her heart to stop pounding. His face was inches away from hers, his breath warming her cheek. She couldn't stop studying the elegant line of his jaw, his throat. Those strong fingers wrapped firmly around her forearm. He couldn't hurt her at least that was certain. Swallowing hard, her thoughts strayed toward giving in.

She definitely had before with men where she was significantly less tempted to do so than this. And despite everything, the intensity in his eyes confirmed something she couldn't deny. Something she knew deep in her bones. That even if this was the last thing she ever did as she lived and breathed...it would be so *very, very good.*

Soleia kicked herself back to reality. *Oh dear god.* What the hell was she thinking?

She pushed away. "NO!"

He crashed onto the sand again. "OW—dammit!"

"Keep your claws to yourself," she huffed, stepping over him before flashing him a facetious grin. "No matter how tempting I know I can be."

Dathon glared as he picked himself up, brushing off the dust and sand again. "Would you stop doing that?" He stilled for a second, cringing as his hand moved to nurse his side. Despite his wound apparently having healed, he was probably still suffering some internal damage.

Observing this, Soleia's shoulders slacked in resignation and she heaved a huge sigh. "Fine! We can share my horse."

He feigned a gracious look, gesturing to the saddle. "So thoughtful." He grunted to pull himself up and forward to grab the reins.

"Hey, it is still my horse," she pointed out. "I get to ride up front."

Dathon rolled his eyes, and waving ceremoniously, he shifted back to give her some space to mount.

She hopped into the saddle and reached to take the reins before sliding back.

He groaned when her rear pressed against him.

Soleia jumped. Evidently, she wasn't the only one riled up from their fight. "M-Maybe you should ride up front." She dismounted quickly and pulled up again to sit behind him.

He was still chuckling when she settled back, clutching at the sides of his shirt.

"You're going to fall off like that," he mused, matter-of-factly.

"Shut up and just go already."

But as soon as Dathon kicked Boots into a canter, she nearly lost her balance, and on instinct, grabbed hold of him.

Another chuckle rumbled through him. And tamping down her groan of resigned exasperation, she shifted closer, winding her arms around his frame, so wide she had to press against his back.

"You are so walking for the next mile," she muttered. She blew out a long, tired breath, gazing out at the darkness of nothing but dunes in all directions. Only Boots' and his occasional huffing disturbed the silence of the night.

They were so far from Ipera. So far from anything she had ever known.

Dathon must have felt her grip slacken, he cleared his throat. "If you fall asleep and fall off, I'm not coming back to get you."

Soleia gritted her teeth and smacked her fist against his torso.

"Ow! You are so violent."

"Speak for yourself," she snapped.

"Hey." He turned his head for a second to glimpse her behind him. "Why do you always carry two swords?"

"I told you it's a style."

He stifled his chuckle, disguising it in clearing his throat again as if he'd already figured there ought to be more to it than that.

"Fine!" Soleia conceded again. "It makes me feel better to have a back-up. It never hurts to have a spare."

He seemed to be satisfied with that, except after a moment, he guessed again, a knowing authority firm in his words. "You don't want to be seen as weak."

Figuring there was no point to confirm his insightful perception, she took a deep breath, settling to watch the tumbleweeds rustle underfoot.

His deep voice rumbled through him. "The world is full of people who would wish to see you fail." He spoke plain, no catch in his tone. "And the best defense is for you to succeed."

Still not responding, she furrowed her eyebrows in disturbed thought, readjusting her head. His heart beat steadily against her ear, through his shirt. Somehow the constant beating soothed her. With his size, he almost blocked her view of where they were going, almost hiding her, almost protecting her. And despite knowing his nature, she felt...unusually safe.

Then Dathon sat up all of sudden.

Soleia blinked. "What's wrong?"

"Shh," he hushed, halting Boots in a flat second and then tilting his head to one side as if straining to hear.

Soleia's eyes narrowed but she couldn't hear anything. The desert sands swirled in a soft shush with the light breeze. Moonlight was shimmering across the sandy landscape—when something large flew past, blocking the light altogether.

Soleia's eyes lit up. "What the hell was that?"

Before Dathon could respond, whatever it was flew past again and knocked both of them off the horse and Boots neighed, rearing back in a startle, stomping his hooves.

Soleia tumbled to the dunes on her back and she caught a glimpse of the shadow of what was flying above them. Her jaw dropped at the sheer size of its wingspan but she couldn't see clearly enough.

Her eyes widened even more when, as she looked past the

flying creature, the faint silhouette of three more of them were circling high in the sky. *Holy shit...*

9

Warrior Mage

Fury etched on his face, Dathon was already on his feet. When one creature dove toward Soleia again, he jumped to cover her, yelling "Watch out!" and they tumbled on the sand.

Several large shadows swooped again. With the darkness helping their concealment, the massive creatures became enveloped in a black smoke just before three solid figures emerged from each inky haze in the form of humans, their faces grim, each of them wearing armored suits with a texture that shimmered in the faint light.

Soleia blinked twice. What did she just see?

Dathon darted to crouch in a defensive position beside her. He glared at the figures beginning to circle the two of them. They were cornered beside a rock formation jutting out of the sand.

One of the prowlers sniffed but didn't say anything.

Dathon growled low in response.

Soleia furrowed her eyebrows in bewilderment, looking from Dathon to the prowlers all of whom were simply glaring wordlessly.

After another moment, Dathon growled again and two of the prowlers pounced on him.

No words. No explanations.

"Boots, hide!" Soleia yelped, prompting the horse to gallop away as she edged backward, leaping to stand up to avoid getting pummelled by the third one and she grunted herself, drawing her swords to retaliate.

The clashing of metal and claws mingled with the desert breeze but nothing else. Soleia panted, still frowning in confusion, even as she charged to strike at her attacker.

Why wasn't anyone speaking? Soleia was baffled. Surely someone ought to have at least accused them of wrongdoing first, assert dominance for the territory, negotiate, make threats, demands—*something*.

Breathless, Soleia jumped back, bracing her side against Dathon's. "Who are these people? What do they want?"

But Dathon roared and before vaulting to fight them all off, he called out, "They want me."

Soleia pursed her lips. She didn't understand what was going on but these people definitely hadn't come to make new friends so she kept on her guard, charging at the prowler closest to her. The spry female tossed her chain whip at Soleia and she cried out as her swords were dragged from her hands. Groaning in annoyance, Soleia launched herself into a spinning kick to knock the female down.

A shadow blocked the moonlight and all of sudden, Soleia's feet lifted from the sand as one of the creatures swooped low to grab her in its talons, nails digging into her shoulders.

Her eyes widened in terror and pain. "Aahh!"

"No!" Dathon launched into a great leap to slash his claw at the creature's feet before it gained altitude.

Screeching at the sting, the creature dropped Soleia with a thud and veered away.

Two of the prowlers seemingly burst into black smoke to circle the skies once more.

Shoulders smarting, stomach churning in dread, Soleia scrambled up to her feet.

Dathon was still fending off another prowler.

The creature that had picked her up landed on the sand some distance away, nursing its wounded claw but it didn't transform. Its black scaly, leathery skin almost gleamed, sharp horns jutting out of its head, red eyes glowing like fire, steam venting from its snout.

Soleia finally saw it clearly and she stammered in disbelief. "A-Are they...dragons?"

She had heard the legends. She had thought they were *mere* legend. A myth.

Dragons were supposed to be rare, malevolent creatures of lore, plundering towns, decimating livestock, and only leaving trails of fiery destruction in their wake. The rest of their nature shrouded in unknowable mystery, left to bedtime stories told to scare little children.

Soleia never thought she'd get to see a real dragon, let alone see real dragons in this sort of close quarters, or bear witness as these mythical dragons shifted into people—people who were trying to kill her.

Dathon was preoccupied fighting off a prowler and when he leaped up to attack, two flying creatures swooped low to charge at him.

Soleia's eyes widened. "NO!" she yelled.

Dathon crashed face first on the sand, incidentally narrowly avoiding getting smashed between the giant beasts. "*Ow—dammit!*"

"You're welcome!" she called out before whirling around to strike at the female prowler again.

Zip! Zip! Zip!

Soleia spun around.

What—?

She dove to dodge whatever was whizzing past them. Her eyes narrowing, she tried to make them out. *Arrows?* "Where are those coming from?"

The creature that had landed on the sand roared upon being hit, two gleaming shafts stuck out from its expansive wing.

The rest of the prowlers in human form alerted as more arrows fell. One of them let out a sharp whistle and in a flat second, they all retreated, disappearing into a thick black haze once more before transforming into their massive dragon forms and taking to the skies to whoosh away and were gone in an instant.

Dathon rushed over to help Soleia up.

Picking up her swords, she met his gaze. "Who the hell were those people?"

He frowned. "That doesn't matter right now. But rest assured, we haven't seen the last of them."

Soleia brushed herself off as she straightened up. "Thank fu—whoa!" Another arrow flew past, just barely missing her face. "What the hell?"

One moment, the desert clearing was empty. Then as though it happened in a split second, they were surrounded by a dozen bandits, desert-dwellers, wearing face coverings and hoods. Several of them holding bows with arrows already cocked, or blunt weapons, daggers, all at the ready.

Dathon held his arm out to keep her behind him. "Stay back."

Soleia pushed it away. "You stay back."

He growled. "Goddammit woman, I am trying to protect you."

"Protect your damn self."

One of the bandits stomped forward from among the others crowding the clearing, even as some of them were also perched against the surrounding rock formation above and around them.

She didn't pull her hood off but Soleia could imagine the bandit was smirking as she examined her shiny blade. "I've never seen those creatures actually land before. Your friend there must be pretty special to them. But you can't save him from us too."

Soleia made a face. "I'm not trying to 'save' him. I want to be the one to kill him." She took a quick step to stand before Dathon and she stuck her chin up, an air of regal authority coming upon her face. "This demon's life is forfeit to me," she declared, her eyes narrowing. "He is *mine*."

The bandit snickered. "Girl, you have no idea what kind of creature you've captured there. His teeth alone would fetch a fortune. Not to mention his eyes or his heart."

"What?" That made her grimace. "How the hell do you know? Are you people cannibals?"

"I'm a hunter," she replied. "A hunter knows game. You have a very rare species of creature. He's going to make all of us very rich. His blood alone contains enough magic to sell. I could bleed him forever and live like a king."

His blood? *Magic?*

An inkling of a thought clicked in Soleia's head.

Her heart pounded in her chest as she strained to clear the fog from her vague recollection of how exactly they had escaped Ipera yesterday—suddenly, inexplicably.

Her hands had been covered in Dathon's blood when she summoned that portal. She looked up to meet the gaze of the hunter warily. "What exactly do you think he is?"

She chucked his chin toward him "He's one of them. That there's a dragon too."

Soleia's eyes widened as it dawned on her.

Dragon.

She turned back slowly to Dathon, his gold-red eyes unwavering. He offered no correction or confirmation but his stubborn chin was set.

Holy shit.

No wonder it seemed as though he understood those creatures that attacked them with no need for words. He was able to communicate with them another way because he was one of them.

Dathon was a dragon.

And—he was the key to unlocking her magic.

Soleia chuckled, shaking her head after a moment before regarding the hunter. "Now I'm definitely not going to let you have him."

"She's pretty cocky," the hunter mocked, turning to the others. "Do you think you can take on all of us, Princess?"

She cringed. "Why are people calling me that?"

Dathon thought to respond. "Maybe because you're a stuck-up witch."

Soleia's indignant response died on her lips as more of the hunters emerged from the shadows and crevices of the rock face.

She stepped back, her grip on her swords tightening.

Dathon surveyed the growing number of emerging hunters and braced his back against hers. Baring his claws again, he glanced sideways. "Are we really going to do this?"

Unflinching, Soleia held her swords out at either side. "Are you scared?"

She almost missed Dathon's low chuckle as the hunter and several of her people squared off around Soleia and Dathon. But before anyone could make the first move, someone called out, "Stop!"

A sharp gust of wind blew everyone back apart, leaving Soleia and Dathon in the middle of their circle as another figure stepped out from behind the rock face.

Breathless, Soleia staggered back to her feet, still in a defensive pose.

The new arrival dispelled the wind he'd conjured and lowered his arms. His head cocked to one side in disbelief. "Soleia...?"

Soleia squinted in bewilderment. "Oh my god, Callan—is that you?" She ran over and threw her arms around his neck.

Dathon's eyebrows jumped up.

The young man laughed and wrapped his beefy arms around Soleia to squeeze her in a happy greeting.

"Look how big you've gotten!" she remarked and he tightened his grip around her, making her feet leave the ground in his embrace while she laughed with him.

"Hey!" Dathon barked.

Soleia glanced back and unwound herself from Callan who gestured to the rest of the hunters with a downward wave of his hand. She sheathed her swords away.

"Naz, she's an old friend," he relayed. "Put it down."

The first hunter's eyes narrowed but she slid her dagger back by her hip before she nodded the signal at everyone else.

"An old friend," Soleia repeated with a highly tickled tone, reaching out to muss up his curly hair. "We grew up together, you rascal."

"What the hell is going on here?" Dathon stepped up, his tone still suspicious.

Soleia grinned. "Callan is from Ipera," she told him. "He's always wanted to be a mage even though he was born into a warrior family. And I'm the opposite!"

Winking, Callan nudged her shoulder. "Two peas in a pod."

She turned a curious look at him. "How did you scare the dragons away?"

"I've enchanted all our arrows."

She gasped in wonder, elbowing him back. "You were always a pretty good caster for a warrior."

Neither Naz nor Dathon were amused by their joyful reunion.

"Enough chatting," Naz interjected. "We should get back to Cavell to sort this out. Sandstorm's coming."

Callan nodded, looking up at the sky to confirm. "You're right."

Naz tilted her head as she walked past. "Brother, I know you've got Therin's ear, you're practically his right hand, but I don't think he'll be very happy about this." She cast a wary glance over at Soleia and Dathon.

"Let me deal with Therin," Callan suggested as they stepped back. "Our horses are stalled behind the edge of this rock," he told Soleia.

One of the hunters was leading Boots back to the group.

Soleia and Dathon both reached for the reins and they looked at each other.

"I ride in front—"

"No, I ride in front—"

"No, I get to ride—"

Naz spat on the ground. "Give these two another god-damned horse."

IO

Cavell

Soleia glanced over her shoulder at Dathon's horse in the middle of the convoy. Naz's men had put iron clamps around his wrists and he was chained to the biggest guy in their group.

She turned to Callan riding beside her. "You call the big guy Hill?"

Callan shrugged. "It's short for Hilario."

"I'll bet," she quipped with a shake of her head. Then her voice barely above a whisper, Soleia added, "You know, those chains aren't necessary." She didn't exactly want to reveal or get into why but she tried to give Callan a reassuring look.

But Callan cast a glance back at Dathon himself before giving Soleia a look. "Oh, yes, they are."

A brisk desert wind whipped now and again, blowing sand everywhere. Soleia already knew she was going to have a hell of a time brushing them out of her hair. But despite the relief upon finding one of her kin, she was still apprehensive.

The rest of the hunters had tried to kill her. Also, she had no idea where they were going.

"So are you going to tell me or do I really need to ask?" was Callan's opening.

Soleia met his gaze. She didn't quite know what to explain first.

"What the hell were you doing riding around the desert with a dragon?"

"We—" She stopped short. "I got lost," she amended. "I'm trying to find my way back to Ipera."

"That's a long way to go, sister. These parts are dangerous. You could have been killed. What were you even thinking?" he hissed in disbelief. "You tried to take on two dozen hunters?" He shook his head. "Then again you never did think before you acted, did you? Your sister would have my head."

Soleia scoffed. "Caelina has enough trouble already. She's pregnant. But it's *your* brother who's being so hormonal."

Callan's jaw dropped. "Oh my god, Stellan is going to be a father! I swear I can't imagine it. That poor child."

She reached over to smack Callan's arm. "What about you? What the hell are you doing all the way out here? When you left, I thought I would never see you again. We all thought you were lost. The estranged son of the Priori."

He gave her a suffering look. "Come on, you and I both know us second-borns can make do better on our own. Besides, you already know what I was looking for."

Her eyes settled evenly on him. "And...did you find it?"

Callan's gaze was distant. "No."

After a moment, someone in the convoy whistled.

"We're here," he noted.

Soleia squinted in the dim as they rode closer. A distinct canyon outline, situated between the mountains, appeared from the darkness up ahead.

"These people have built an entire community within these rock mountains across the desert and have been living here for at least a generation."

The cool air wafted out of the gaping entryway into the giant cave gouged into the mountain. Several desert people stood guard by the doorway. Embellishments and sculptures had been carved into the face of the canyon.

The convoy rode past a few structures right outside the caves and Soleia could imagine that the place must function as a square or market during the day. If Callan was right, there could be hundreds of people living within these mountains.

She furrowed her eyebrows, noting some distinctly different physical attributes as she watched several citizens pass them by closer to the entrance. She turned to Callan with a hushed whisper of marveling, "Are they humans?"

"Some of them."

"I was told there weren't any humans south of the Semi River."

Callan simply shrugged. "I think we weren't told many things back in Ipera."

Soleia shivered at the truth of that but she shook it off.

"You can leave your horse here. The hunters will take care of Boots," Callan instructed after dismounting.

He led the way through the entrance and after a mere few steps, they arrived at a large cavern with a high ceiling that was lit up by several lamps and torches mounted against the walls.

A magnificent natural structure, several narrow crevices, and tunnels had been meticulously dug into the inner walls at different points along the back which Soleia assumed led to different areas of the community.

Soleia's eyes were wide. She watched as both human and Fae warriors sat together, talking, laughing, and sharing meals, and even in the lateness of the hour with the mere handful of people awake, the community seemed vibrant and alive. "Callan, this is truly amazing."

The first large cavern served as a resting or refreshment area. Dusty benches flanked long wooden tables where a handful of the hunters from earlier had taken a load off and were passing around jugs of drinks, plates of bread, and steaming, charred vegetables.

"Have a seat." Callan gestured to the nearest table. "I'm guessing you could do with some proper food. I know I certainly could."

The rest of the hunting party had scattered away to their own business, possibly headed to rest after the long night or going home to family.

Dathon was being dragged away by the big guy toward the back of the cavernous ridge, followed by three more hunters.

Soleia met his gold-red gaze for a brief moment before she turned to Callan. "Where are they taking him?"

Callan's eyebrow rose. "Are you worried about the dragon?"

Soleia couldn't help the unease nagging in the back of her mind. She had established a deal with Dathon. But she also couldn't help Callan's people's completely justified wariness of him.

She scoffed, trying instead for nonchalance. "On the

contrary, I think you've sent too few guards. He's going to try to escape. He's been nothing but trouble so far."

"We don't have a dungeon as such, but our hunters are well-trained. They'll be on top of things," he assured.

"I think it will be better if he's where I can keep an eye on him. I can't explain right now but would you just trust me on this? Please?" she implored, her eyebrows raised.

Callan's eyes narrowed for a moment but he signaled a nod to Hill who shoved Dathon to slump down to sit on a flat rock at the end of the room with a clear view from them before stepping away.

Sliding into the seat, Soleia unstrapped her double blade scabbard and propped it against the table by her leg just as a rotund man came through with a tray of goblets and jugs.

He handed Callan a set with a short nod before moving through the rest of the tables of people having returned from the hunt.

"Thank you." Callan turned to hand Soleia a goblet of drink. "Here, try this."

After one sip, Soleia's eyes widened in recognition and shock. "Is this...? How did you get elven mead all the way out here?"

"There's a market that sells similar ingredients." Grinning, he tipped his cup toward her. "Here's to home."

Soleia smiled in pleasure as she gulped it all down and then eagerly refilled her goblet.

"Callan, brother," the first hunter from earlier, Naz greeted them cheerily as she arrived, clapping her hand on Callan's back before swinging her leg over the bench, the wood nearly creaking in complaint as she sat down. Her browned complexion, masculine jaw, and dark eyes were no longer covered by her hood and face covering. "Maybe now that we're not trying to kill each other, your lovely friend would like an introduction."

Soleia grimaced at her. "Not really."

Naz spun around to reach for a plate of food from the next table. Was it even hers? She plunked it before her and started eating it anyway

Callan laughed. "Soleia, this is Naz. She's a righteous felon but she's saved my life more times in the last two years than I can count."

"As have you." She tilted her head to acknowledge before looking Soleia up and down again. "So...was she your girl-friend back home or something?"

Soleia and Callan both laughed.

Soleia thumped her fist on his shoulder. "I think I'm not going to dignify that with an answer."

Naz shook her head. "Well, in that case, I'm sure Therin will be very curious as to why you were willing to spare her life—and the dragon's."

Callan pursed his lips. "They'll be back in the morning, won't they?"

Naz merely nodded since she was stuffing her mouth full of bread.

At Callan's worried tone, Soleia's eyebrows furrowed. "This Therin guy sounds like a charmer," she noted. "How did you get mixed up with these people anyway?"

Callan was eager to defend them. "If it wasn't for these guys, I would have been dragon food as well. In the two years I've been here, I've made many good friends. It's a struggle to live in the desert but they're accustomed to it. They wouldn't live anywhere else. They're good people."

A pretty young human woman wearing a long flowy shift came by to refill the jugs. She smiled at Callan who acknowledged her with a nod and a "Thank you" before she strolled past them to do the same to the other tables.

Amused by that, Soleia turned to watch his face. "Good people indeed. And do you have a special someone among these good people?"

And Callan's cheeks reddened.

Naz laughed out loud, spurting out crumbs. "Callan? That'll be the day, eh, friend?" She pounded on Callan's back in good humor.

"Point being." Callan gave her a pointed look before meeting Soleia's gaze again. "These people saved my life. I owe them. And Therin finds me useful."

"Useful enough to let a dragon live?" Naz mumbled through another mouthful.

"Therin is a rational man," Callan noted. "He will understand if I explain."

Still chewing, Naz was staring back at Dathon as though appraising him from afar. "His kind is definitely rare. Dragons are the hunter's ultimate prize."

Soleia's eyebrows furrowed in curiosity. "Have you ever caught one?"

She shook her head. "Not me. Not yet. I've only heard the stories from Therin. I heard one dragon skeleton they found in the desert fetched so much gold, the yield sustained the community for eight seasons." She shrugged, shoveling food around her plate with her fingers. "That was decades ago though. To tell the truth of it, these dragons are tricky. It's quite rare to see even one of them so far from the den."

Callan turned to Soleia. "The dragons have a den over by the next ridge. We believe their nest is close to the Outlands so the den must be where they keep their hoard this side of the continent."

"Their hoard?" Soleia repeated.

"Ah yes, the fabled dragon hoard," Naz concurred. "Therin always talks about that. It's almost certain there's a hoard of gold at the den that can sustain the community for a year. Having said that, I can't even imagine how big the hoard is that they must be keeping at the nest."

"Enough to feed the community for ten generations," Callan guessed with a shrug.

"It wouldn't have been such a big deal," Naz told Soleia, "but in recent years, it's been getting harder and harder to sustain the desert crops with magic alone, and every year, the hunting grounds get scarcer and further away. And every year, the dragons terrorize a new community, stealing valuable resources to supply their nest."

Her curiosity piqued, Soleia wanted to know. "Where is this nest?"

Callan shrugged again. "Nobody knows. Rumors say it's past the edge of the world."

Naz huffed, tossing a glance over at Dathon again. "I suppose it's no trouble if you've got wings."

Soleia followed his gaze. "You think he knows where it is?"

But Callan was already resolved. "If he did, he'll never say."

* * *

Naz and Callan had settled into a different conversation when Soleia stepped away. She walked over toward the captive dragon, shrouded in a dark cloud, his face sour as he maintained his sulk.

"Here." She handed Dathon a cup of the elven mead as she sat down beside him on the flat rock.

Dathon sneered, turning his back to her. "I'm not drinking that."

She rolled her eyes. "Fine." She gulped it down instead.

"I don't like this," he muttered. "We shouldn't stay here."

"I told you it's fine," she exhaled in exasperation.

"These people tried to kill us." He darted a glance back at her.

She shrugged. "We're in a truce. Besides, Callan is one of my people."

"Not anymore from the looks of it," he argued, keeping his voice low. "You don't know where his loyalties lie. We need to get out of here. I thought you wanted to go back to Ipera?"

"Jeez, I also want a nice place to rest for the night," she declared. "I don't know about you but I'm exhausted and I sure would appreciate not having to sleep on the ground."

Dathon huffed but said nothing.

"I wouldn't be opposed to some fresh clothes either," she remarked, moving to remove her cloak as the air inside the cavern was warmer than the exposed desert. But when she shifted her shoulder, she hissed from the sting. She had almost forgotten that she'd injured it when the dragons from earlier had grabbed and tried to fly away with her.

Dathon surged up in his seat, already heaving. "How bad is it? Does it still hurt? Those bastards."

She had started to dismiss him, "It's just a scratch. It'll heal," before she met his intense gaze.

There seemed to be more than rage simmering beneath Dathon's eyes, more than anger for the enemy he couldn't reach for the moment, his face darkening with something akin to remorse.

But it was gone as fast as it came.

Convinced her exhaustion was simply playing on her senses, Soleia turned her attention to the iron around Dathon's wrists restricting his movement. "I'll talk to Callan about the clamps again."

He grumbled in displeasure. "So we *are* prisoners?"

"No." She shook her head before stopping to consider. "Maybe..."

He held up his hands. "They put me in chains."

She gave him a pointed look. "Can you blame them? They can't risk a dangerous creature like you on the loose among their people."

Growling low, he huffed again, looking away.

Despite herself, she cracked a small smirk. "I honestly thought you would try to beat down the guards and escape the first chance you got."

"I thought about it," he admitted before turning to meet her gaze again. "But I need you, don't I? I may have clamps on my wrists but this is my real prison." He tugged at the string of beads around his neck.

Soleia's stomach churned, almost in guilt, but she steadied

her chin. "On that score, there's no one else to blame but yourself."

He didn't respond.

A bit wary, she tilted her head. "So are you really a dragon? Or what are you?"

"You wouldn't understand," he grumbled.

She took a deep breath. "I suppose a dragon could indeed lay waste to entire continents fairly easily. That must be the destruction Oma spoke of." She shook her head. "I'd never seen my grandmother so afraid of anything in my entire life. Even the giant wraith didn't faze her as much as you did."

"I knew you wouldn't understand," he scoffed. "You tricky Fae and your irresponsible use of magic. The arrogance of some beings is just unconscionable. I should have let your entire village burn down. I should have killed you when I had the chance."

At the change in his manner, her chest tightened, and she narrowed her eyes. "You can't threaten me. Now that I know I've got a use for you."

"Ah, of course," he drawled with a sly grin. "You need dragon blood to coax your pathetic magic to come out. And I suppose you expect now your family will finally accept you?" He leaned closer to speculate himself, "How much of my blood do you think you'll need to make your family happy? Are you going to bleed me dry too?"

She clenched her jaw at his callous tone. "If you don't stop annoying me, maybe I will!" She was intending to get up and stalk off but he grabbed her arm, his irons clanking loudly.

"Soleia," Callan called out from across the room, beckoning her over.

Her gaze snapped up to meet Callan's and she nodded in response. She glared back at Dathon and when she shrugged him off, he yielded, dropping his hands. "I suggest you get some rest. And you'd better not make any trouble for me for the entire night." She stood up to follow Callan but stopped in mid-stride at Dathon's blunt question.

"Are you going to bed with him?"

"What?" Her eyes popped wide.

Dathon raised his eyebrows but didn't repeat it.

Soleia's cheeks burned but she tried to keep glaring at him. "Again, that's none of your business."

"I wouldn't say so."

She shot him a skeptical look of disbelief.

He rolled his eyes and clarified his point. "I only mean these people are strangers. Right now, from where I'm sitting, they're holding us captive. You should be careful who you trust."

"Callan is like a brother to me," Soleia pointed out.

His eyes narrowed before uttering his grave, potent response, "Sometimes, even family can deceive you."

11

Community

In the light of the early morning, the open area right outside the caves transformed into a lively market square, just as
Soleia had guessed. Amidst the reds and browns of the desert,
the colorful people of Cavell turned out to commune.

An elderly lady was constantly churning out food to share
from a smoking grill beneath one rickety stand. A handful
of children were running around with makeshift kites, others
playing with stones on the sandy ground.

Beside a cart of brightly colored fabric, another small
crowd of children and their parents were gathered before
Callan who was amusing them with a bit of magical illusion,
conjuring a hazy swarm of blue butterflies fluttering about
his hands before turning them into green butterflies before
turning them into a shower of confetti.

Soleia couldn't help a smile at the wonder in the eyes of
his audience, the genuineness of the children's giggles, and the

open trust in everyone's faces. She envied Callan somewhat. He never seemed to have trouble blending in with different kinds of people, whereas she had always tended to stick out— an outsider, even among her peers.

Despite her impatience to find a way home, Soleia found the new and different culture intriguing. She had never been outside Ipera. It was refreshing to be around friendly people who had no preconceived notions of her. She could be herself. Perhaps try to belong.

With that recourse, somehow, she had found herself seated in a circle of citizens, going through a pile of clothing that needed mending. Holding up a child-sized tunic that needed to be let out, Soleia made a face. "Am I doing this right?"

Mayu, one of the human citizens sitting nearest to Soleia, turned to inspect her uneven stitching. Trying to stifle a giggle, she blinked. "Oh, dear, um." She gave Soleia a kind smile. "I think perhaps Hano should show you again the best way to do it."

Cheeks reddening, Soleia cringed. "I'm so sorry, Mayu." She looked around the group with admiration. "I have yet to develop the expertise with needles that you all have." She picked up another item of clothing with an embroidered design from the pile. "And the detail on some of these is just lovely."

Mayu's smile widened. "We each have our own skills. A society is not built of all blacksmiths or seamstresses. Besides, it is the mere willingness to lend a hand that enriches the community spirit."

"Thank you for saying that but I think perhaps I will try again when I am assured not to hinder your efforts." Soleia let out a sheepish chuckle, giving Mayu's shoulder a soft pat before she moved to straighten up, dusting off her hands.

"Soleia."

Soleia turned and beamed a greeting at the seamstress whom Callan had recommended to supply her with clothes as she approached. "Aletha."

Aletha shifted the infant baby bundled against her chest with the sturdy piece of cloth before greeting with, "Does the dress fit well?"

"Yes, it's absolutely divine." She smoothed down the scoop neck dress with the gathered skirt; its loose, light fabric was perfect for the climate, and it matched the bandanna she had found to protect her hair. "Thank you so much."

Shiny square tiles of a necklace jangling around Aletha's neck caught Soleia's eyes. "That is gorgeous."

"Thank you." Aletha smiled. "It's made of dragon scales. It's very rare." She repeated it to her baby who was trying to grab it. "That's very rare, my love." But then she shook her head knowing it was a futile reprimand before prompting Soleia again, "So, you're a mage from Callan's village too?"

"That's right."

Aletha's eyes widened. "And you can do the same casting as Callan? That's amazing!"

Hiding a grimace, Soleia fidgeted in her stance. "Um...sort of. I'm not as good as him though." Despite their having been two peas in a pod growing up, each wanting the life of the other, Soleia had never been brave enough to tell Callan the truth about her magic before either, or lack thereof.

"Still likely a great deal better than any of us," Aletha

guessed, gesturing around them. "The call of magic has weakened around these parts lately. Not many Fae in Cavell can access the gift and we no longer train and practice as we used to do. Callan is blessed to have honed his skills thus far. We for sure would not know what to do without him."

Soleia smiled. "I am glad Callan has found his place here with your people."

"Yes, he has been very helpful. He is also very kind," Aletha relayed. "I have heard that the old Fae have no great sympathy for humans."

It was true. Soleia had never even seen or spoken to a human until yesterday. It wasn't that the non-magical beings were seen as a threat, but rather more inconsequential. "I didn't realize how similar humans are to us."

Aletha nodded. "Here in the community, we are all kin. No matter the shape of our ears, our statures, our abilities— now more so than before. We no longer think of ourselves apart. I am only one among a few of the first Fae born here. My parents said they were mages, come from a village just east of Ipera, near the foothills of the ranges."

Her mouth parted in wonder. "I see. Have you ever tried to go back?"

"I did once when I was younger," she confessed. "I wanted to try to find more of our people. But the western mountain range becomes treacherous during certain seasons. So much so that others have speculated there may be some form of magic at work. Nobody I know has ever made it there and back."

Soleia's eyebrows furrowed at a tremor of unease. It almost sounded like Aletha was saying there was no way to go back to the Fae lands from here.

But Soleia dismissed that thought. That would have been years ago. And Aletha had said it herself. The desert mages were largely untrained, lacking impetus, and unlike Soleia, they had no access to dragon blood—such potent magic should certainly overcome.

"But no matter," Aletha dismissed with a soft smile on her face as she surveyed their surroundings. "I am happy here. We have everything we need."

Folding her arms across her chest, Soleia cast her eyes around her too, taking in the colors and vibrance of the desert community. She could certainly see the appeal it held. However, from the previous evening's discussions with Naz and Callan regarding what was required to sustain the community, Soleia had a feeling it was a lot more complicated than Aletha was aware of.

A figure sauntering out of the dim canyon entryway caught Soleia's eyes.

Dathon had also been provided with a change of clothes. He no longer wore the bloodstained and torn top from yesterday and his face was freshly washed. His eyes were darting around as if in search of something, his tall, forbidding form already making other passers-by steer wide clear of him.

Soleia was busy admiring the way his new tunic shirt clung to his torso in places as the wind gusted past his form, it took her a moment to realize he probably didn't recognize her in the new clothes either. She raised her hand to catch his eye.

When he spotted her, his eyes narrowed, his steps purposefully headed in her direction and something about the way he stalked toward her made her pulse quicken.

She almost gasped when he finally towered over her,

standing a mere few inches away, even more when his eyes roved over her in the new dress. It was as if he was running his eyes over each stitch, each crease, each curve. His chest rose and fell at his appraisal.

It was clear he liked what he saw, a low growl rumbled out of him. She wasn't even sure if he noticed it himself but it shot a thrill right through her anyway.

She swallowed hard when his brilliant gold-red gaze lifted to meet hers. Something in his eyes made her flush hot. It was the same look he'd had in the desert after their tussle—a want, a need. Except now she felt the stir within herself.

She tried not to make her question sound too breathy, "Where have you been?"

He grunted in displeasure, the heat in his eyes dissipating slightly. "Your 'good friend' has only just ordered his men to unchain me and my neck is sore from sleeping on that rock," he muttered. Then his tone changed to add, "I suppose *you* had a good night."

Soleia casually tilted her head slightly to consider. "Yes, actually, it was the best sleep I've had in a long time."

Dathon's prompt was dry. "Just sleep?"

Bemused, Soleia turned to meet his eyes again. The intensity was back in them. But before she could repeat that it wasn't any of his business, a commotion erupting from the entrance to the canyon grabbed her attention.

About a dozen horses were riding in, noisy hooves and neighing echoing throughout the canyon.

Readying her stance in case it was some sort of attack, Soleia braced her hand almost instinctively to keep Dathon back, moving to reach back for her swords only to wince at the recollection that Callan had *made* her leave her swords with Boots at the stables for the morning market.

She'd seriously almost had to fight him tooth and nail to keep them too. But she was technically an outsider and even the community had its rules. Not to mention they didn't really go with her new dress. Instead, her hand slid down to feel for the hidden dagger strapped against her thigh for a brief reassurance.

But the people of the community rushed to greet the incoming team of horses. As the group rode closer, it appeared each rider wore the same clothing as the citizens of Cavell, and each horse was loaded with packs of fabric, sacks of food, tools, animal carcasses, and supplies for the season. It was their hunters' triumphant return.

At that conclusion, Soleia's stance relaxed, only to stiffen again as the burly man who looked to be leading the arriving team pinned his gaze on her—or right just about above her shoulder.

The man with long salt-and-pepper hair and inked marks across both his tanned, muscled forearms must have been the leader of their people whom Callan was talking about. His keen experienced hunter instincts likely already detected that the creature standing right behind Soleia was neither Fae nor human.

Callan was promptly by her side by the time Therin galloped to an abrupt stop a few feet away from her but Soleia stood her ground, not even wincing except to blink away the dust his horse had kicked up from her eyes.

Therin dismounted with a loud thud, his heavy gait an easy signal that he wasn't entirely welcoming of intruders in his community.

But Callan was on point. "Soleia, this is Therin." He made a sweeping gesture of his arm. "He leads the hunters in this community." He glanced up toward the burly man. "Therin, this is Soleia. She's from my village, the Priori Fae clan of the western mountain ranges."

But Therin's sharp gaze shifted to Dathon standing behind her.

"And that's a dragon."

<h1 style="text-align:center">12</h1>

<h1 style="text-align:center">Untapped</h1>

Therin's eyes lit up in alert, already drawing his dagger, prompting a handful of his men to hasten to do so as well. "Why the hell isn't it in chains?"

"Whoa, whoa, whoa, hey—" Soleia jumped in front of Dathon and put her hands up for everyone to calm down. "He won't harm anyone." She gestured to Callan. "Callan can attest that the dragon poses no danger right now." She stuck her chin up. "I am responsible for him."

The old hunter's eyes narrowed in suspicion but after a nod of confirmation from Callan, and a very, *very* long moment of consideration, Therin's posture relaxed and he sheathed his weapon.

He regarded Soleia with a halfway incredulous look. "Do you command this beast?"

"In a manner of speaking."

Therin sniffed as though he could discern the truth from

107

her scent or the dragon's. He took a deep breath and squared his shoulders as if in wary apprehension then he waved his hand to yell out his instructions to the returning team, "Pack it away!"

Callan was chewing on his inner cheek. "Shall we all take a seat inside and rest? Judging from the loot, your mission has been fruitful."

But Therin's forehead was creased as though he was pondering something. He cracked his neck. "No time to rest. This day might turn out even more fruitful than I'd thought." He beckoned Callan to follow as he strode off. "Bring her. We must prepare."

Grimacing, Soleia stepped back. "I won't be 'brought' anywhere."

Coming up from behind, Hill grabbed her arm.

"Hey!" She tried to shrug him off but Hill was an immovable pillar—an immovable pillar who had drawn a dagger to her neck.

Beside her, another two hunters had grabbed an indignant Dathon.

Soleia shot Callan a stunned look but his eyes were wide as he stood frozen. He had obviously erroneously expected a more welcoming reception from Therin.

She glanced over at Dathon whose eyebrows were already furrowed.

He had been correct last night.

Therin's arrival had certainly made one thing clear.

They were prisoners.

Therin led the way toward the large pale tent that had been set up at the end of the gorge. The thick, canvas material billowed in the breeze wending through the canyon. He stopped at the door, his finger pointing at Dathon. "The creature stays outside."

Soleia met Dathon's incensed gaze before Hill dragged her into the tent with the others, leaving Dathon by the tent entryway flanked by three big hunters.

Lit by the brightness of the desert sun, the inside of the tent was sparse. Map scrolls and yellowed paper parchment were strewn across one wooden table, the papers held down by large rocks and half-melted candles in stone bowls. On another table to one side were drink goblets and different-sized glass jars and vials stashed for a purpose Soleia could not determine.

Therin walked up to the central table and shook a pile of papers to pull out one of the maps. "One of our scouts got word that the leader of the dragon's den will be departing at sundown tonight to go back to the nest. He should be gone for a good few hours which gives us enough time."

Soleia looked from him to the others. "Time for what?"

Naz's grin was wide. "Time to strike."

"Strike what...?"

"What do you think?"

Soleia was already making a face. "Are you going to try to capture a dragon?"

Therin's dagger glare pierced her. "A dragon is the hunter's ultimate prize. There's usually only one caught every generation. Imagine if we caught more. Every part of it is precious. We could just piecemeal sell it off and make so much gold."

Indignant, Soleia gritted her teeth, her stomach churning. "But aren't they also people?"

Therin huffed. "You Fae and your pity for monsters." He cast a glance over at Callan as though he had noted this before. "But I suppose today is your lucky day." He turned his attention back to the map. "My next mark isn't a dragon but a treasure they've come to possess. There has been talk of a legendary artifact. It's supposed to be the most powerful object in the land, and with all magic being volatile of late, it might be our only hope. My boy Callan here says it could well serve as a never-ending source of energy for the community."

He straightened up, folding his arms across his chest. "Matter of fact, I can imagine there will be all sorts of treasures these dragons have hoarded at the den. I reckon it should be enough to last the community for a good long spell."

Enthused about the news, Naz clapped her hand on Callan's back. "I'm sure there will be loot enough for everyone there. Dragons love to hoard."

Soleia frowned. The last thing she needed right now was to get involved in a conflict between the desert hunters and the dragons. She shook her head. "I'm not going to be a part of whatever you're thinking. This has got nothing to do with me."

Therin tilted his head. "On the contrary, we've been planning this attack for nearly two seasons and here you show up at the most opportune time. An advantage we've never had before. A mage with a captive dragon. He could tell us everything we need to know to make our mission a success." He flashed a wily grin. "I think that's what you could call fate."

"Call it what you want, I'm not doing it," Soleia sneered.

Therin whirled to peer closer at Soleia, she almost flinched. He reeked of sun and sweat and the wrinkles on his browned face deepened as his eyes narrowed. "The arrogance of the old Fae," he drawled. "Were you under the impression that I'm giving you a choice?"

His rank breath right in her face, Therin's hardened glower made to cut her down. "I spend my days hunting vicious beasts, little girl. If you think I'm going to blink twice killing the likes of you just because of your old friend, you are gravely mistaken." His grin turned sly. "Or there's the door. You're welcome to try to fight your way out of my canyon. Sometimes I like it when they run." He met Hill's laughing gaze by the entryway before he faced the table once more with a grunt. "In the meantime, I have mouths to feed."

Soleia turned aghast eyes to Callan but the disturbed look on his face as he chewed his bottom lip only made her queasier.

Callan may not have liked Therin's methods but he was also concerned for the citizens. "It is a very rare occasion when the leader of the den flies back to the nest. We likely won't have an opportunity like this again before the cold descends."

Naz was glaring at Dathon's figure shadowed right outside the tent entryway. "What if the dragon could fly in unnoticed? He's one of them. That could be our in."

Therin's eyebrow rose in intrigue at her suggestion and he stomped outside again.

Soleia met Callan's wary gaze again before running out after him.

Dathon's expression was half-bored, half-affronted as Therin looked him up and down in appraisal.

Therin raised his hand to wave instruction at Soleia. "Command him to shift."

"Shift? You mean change into a dragon?" Soleia's gaze darted up to Dathon's for a second. "Oh, uhh...he...can't right now."

"Why the hell not?"

"Um, well..." She hesitated, cracking her neck in strain and almost embarrassment. "When I said I commanded him, the truth is... He's been...cursed." She turned to Callan as the most likely one of them to understand. "The dragon's spirit has been bound so he can't exactly shift."

Therin's eyes narrowed again. "Bound? Bound how? And by what?"

Her eyebrows lifting, Soleia turned toward Dathon again in a sort of prompt. There was only one easy way to explain—certainly one most entertaining one. And it had seemed to simply deter him more than injure him in any case.

But Dathon gave her an alarmed knowing look. "Don't."

Soleia bit her lip and took a deep breath. "NO."

And Dathon crashed face first to the ground. "Ow—dammit!"

The two hulking guards flanking him stepped back in surprise. Naz just outright burst out laughing and slapped her thigh in mirth.

Dathon picked himself up off the ground, his smoldering glare searing into Soleia's impish grimace.

Therin merely looked amused, though not amused enough to be happy that he couldn't access the full power of the dragon right then. "A dragon in its human form and his weak female mage master," he remarked with a shake of his head. "I've never seen two more useless creatures before."

That set Soleia off and she snarled.

Callan had to hold her arm to restrain her from pouncing on Therin. "We could still use them," he insisted, matter-of-factly. He probably knew Therin disposed of things that were *not* useful to him. "Soleia is a portal summoner."

Soleia's heart dropped to her toes, her struggle ceasing in an instant.

Oh shit. Here we go.

Callan turned to regard Therin and Naz with a look. "In the past, every time we tried to take the den, the dragons could always smell us or hear us from miles away. But if we had a portal summoner, we might finally have the element of surprise on our side." He finished with a big smile.

"That's right!" Naz chimed in. "If they can sneak into the dragon's den, disarm a few guards, and then give a signal, we can all ride in and take the hoard."

This time when Soleia slid her gaze over to Dathon's, he was already giving her a bemused pointed look.

Oohh shit.

She couldn't let them plan this. She especially couldn't let them plan this and have everyone's safety, *everything*, riding on her so-called abilities.

"Wait, wait, wait—" Soleia put her hand up.

"What? What is it now?" Therin wanted no more interruptions.

She pursed her lips, her gaze on the ground. "I'm-I'm sorry. Callan has misunderstood. I'm not a portal summoner."

"What?" Callan's forehead creased.

She gave him a sheepish look to explain. "When we were children, that—that was just a fluke. I'm *not* a portal summoner," she declared. "I just can't do it again. I never could.

I really am so sorry." She couldn't stand the puzzled, disappointed look on Callan's face. She dropped her gaze again.

But Therin's eyes narrowed in suspicion. "You're lying. A weakling like you, there's no way you have made it here on one horse with limited supplies from the western ridge without using portals."

"Yeah, how did you get here anyway?" Naz interjected.

Soleia rolled her shoulders. "It was an accident!"

Therin waved impatiently. "Then have another accident!"

Soleia distressed. "I-I can't. I can barely..."

"Soleia..." Callan put a hand on her shoulder in sympathy.

"You don't even have magic?" Therin's face was red with pent-up rage.

Naz shot him a wary look before glaring back at Soleia again. "Come on, girl. You're not doing yourself any favors here," she mocked pointedly. "Talented little Fae mages like you, with a little more practice, some magic enhancers, some runes, some spices—"

Callan nodded as he chimed in. "Aletha has amulets, whatever, just tell us what you need—"

Still cringing, Soleia followed him with her gaze as he anxiously paced back and forth doing an inventory of magical ingredients. His only way of fighting for her was to satisfy Therin. But suffice it to say, Soleia had already tried every kind of magical stimulant to induce her powers in the past to no avail. She wanted to explain it was impossible but they all seemed decided, determined, to find an alternative.

She already knew there wasn't one. There was only one thing she needed to make it work. The only one thing that had *ever* made it work.

Therin huffed and he chucked his chin as a signal to Hill. "Kill the dragon. We'll just take the blood."

Soleia's jerked in alarm. "Wait, wait, wait!" She put her hands up. "His—his blood," she spoke up almost helplessly. "His blood makes my magic work."

Therin's eyes lit up almost savagely. "Done." And with no warning whatsoever, out of nowhere, he whipped a blade toward Dathon, slicing deep into his arm, precious dragon blood gushing deep red onto the dusty ground.

"Aagh—!" Dathon collapsed to his knees.

"Dathon!" Soleia cried out, rushing over to him before darting a glare back at Therin over her shoulder. "For god's sake, I didn't need that much!"

Hiding a small grin, Therin shrugged. "Sorry, my mistake."

Frantic, Soleia scanned around for something that she could use to mend his wound or at least collect the blood. None of the other hunters were much concerned, alarmed, or surprised.

Grimacing, Callan spun his hand and a small glass vial flitted from the table inside the tent and into his grasp. He reached out to hand it to Soleia. "Here."

With one hand putting pressure on the gash to keep Dathon from bleeding out, Soleia grabbed the vial to collect the fresh blood. "Do you have any bandages or cloth?" she urged.

"I want to see the magic now," Therin pressed, his tone brooking no refusal.

Soleia shot him the dirtiest of looks. It seemed Callan had severely mischaracterized Therin as being a 'rational man.' Deeply regretting she didn't have her swords with her, she gritted her teeth instead as she straightened up, dropping the vial. She didn't need it. Dragon blood dripped from her fingers.

She clasped her hands together and closed her eyes for a moment. She was so pissed off that she was instantly emotionally connected to her magic and it ignited an instinct within her which arose easier than she'd expected.

She tried to remember the simplest spell, the first air spell they had all been taught. She breathed out slowly and opened her eyes. She clasped her fists together before separating her palms, her fingers spread wide.

And when Soleia called upon the wind, just like the last time she had tried right before the feast at Ipera, something surged inside her.

But unlike the last time she had tried, a force manifested between her hands, and a tingling ran up her arms, coursing through her body, the energy of the magic reaching inside her, permeating everywhere. It was warm, soothing, as if a vague aching deep inside her she didn't even know was there was instantly eased.

The slight desert breeze winding through the canyon intensified almost instantly, building into a gale-force wind that whipped at everyone's clothes and hair. It swirled around Soleia's form and she squinted while the sands shook around them.

Callan was holding down the tent flaps flying crazily about even as his mouth opened in wonderment at the display.

Another gesture with her hands and everyone around her was blown staggering back a step by a sharp gust, similar to what Callan had used to break up the fight when he had first encountered them.

Regaining his footing, Therin's eyebrows rose in approval.

Heaving, Soleia beamed in pleasure. The entire length of her arms tingled with vibrations. It was the first time that she had conjured *anything*. Her chest felt full and, for once in her life, she felt a semblance of purpose. All those years of feeling weak, perhaps she wasn't as useless as she thought, as everyone thought, after all.

Somewhat proud of herself, she looked over to meet Dathon's gaze. He was still crouched on the ground. He didn't look at all pleased and he was still clutching at his bleeding arm.

Her smile fading, Soleia's magic fizzled out and she dropped her hands.

But Therin was finally happy. "Alright then," he concluded. "That was no portal but it's proof you're not completely useless." He clapped his hands before he spun to leave. "We'll depart at sundown. We can't risk delaying this sort of mission."

"Sundown?" Soleia stammered. "A bit of wind might be simple but portal summoning is the rarest and most difficult form of casting. I can't guarantee you I can call portals by sundown."

Therin glanced back with a nonchalant look. "Well then, you've got all day to control your 'gift.' Otherwise, we'll bleed your dragon dry and use the magic ourselves. My boy Callan here can do magic too." He tilted his head. "He'll probably need more of your dragon's blood of course but that's no skin off my back."

It wasn't exactly encouraging or inspiring. Soleia seethed but could only watch them go. And with only a hesitant glimpse back at her, Callan followed Therin and the others back toward the market and the cave entryway.

She let out a frustrated groan and went to Dathon's side. "Are you okay?"

Dathon was heaving, his teeth clenched as he tried to focus away from the pain.

Guilt gnawing on her insides, she almost couldn't bear seeing him in agony, almost couldn't bear to see him so beat down and defenseless. It was as if he was a mere ghost of his former self—the strong and capable creature she knew he was.

And it was all her fault.

"Dathon..." She cupped his cheek, lifting his face.

Blazing rage flashed in his gold-red eyes but as soon as his gaze met hers, it flickered, softening in an instant.

Soleia was at a loss for words but her concern must have been plain on her face, her own indignation and anguish as if somehow his pain was hers too.

The small movement of his head was to turn his jaw into her touch, his lower lip grazing her palm, his eyes closing for a moment as her hand warmed his cheek.

Her chest aching, Soleia couldn't help but stroke his face with her fingers.

Callan was rushing back toward them with bandages. "In here," he beckoned them to return to the tent to shelter from the heat.

"Thank you." But Soleia couldn't keep the remorse and bitterness out of her tone.

"I'm really sorry about Therin. He's a lot rough around the

edges," Callan admitted, his face still cringed. "Nothing quite like today. But times are getting desperate."

Soleia tossed Callan a cautious look while she tended to Dathon's arm. "That brute saved your life?"

Callan blinked before nodding.

She pursed her lips. "Let's hope that debt does not bind you forever, brother."

* * *

13

Risks

Soleia had found a quiet corner past the market, near the entrance to the canyon, to practice her magic. She didn't want to accidentally hurt anyone if she screwed up any spells. Not even counting Caelina's almost torching her pet uquix, Soleia had seen spells gone badly before. Tobias was always causing weather disturbances, and one time, Anelis had accidentally turned everything in the village square yellow. It had taken ages for the color to scrub off. Soleia clearly remembered because the three of them had been tasked to clean it up—without using magic.

She almost couldn't believe she was here again. She had to perform her stupid magic or die of humiliation. But this time she had to summon a portal by sundown or she would just actually be killed.

Her feet planted in a stance, Soleia stood with her arms folded at her elbows, her palms hovering close together, her eyes closed. She took a deep breath, feeling the energy swirl inside her before she moved to push both palms forward.

She opened her eyes slowly to see a bit of rock from a few feet away crumble and collapse onto the sand. But no portal.

It had been *hours* but still—no portal.

She dropped her hands in exasperation. "Dammit!"

Treating the dragon blood between her fingertips and positioning to try again, she squeezed her eyes shut to concentrate on Oermilla's teachings, trying to remember her droning words, all the while regretting all over again how she had never really paid attention to her casting training.

Portal summoning is about making unseen worlds seen, making what's intangible tangible... You need to feel what's around you, see through its eyes, hear music in the silence...

Sweat dripped from her scalp and the hot haze prickled her skin.

Come on, dammit. Just one. PLEASE.

Clenching her teeth so hard she thought she might bleed herself, she let out a short grunt as she pushed her hands forward again.

Nothing.

With a frustrated yell, she stamped her feet, wildly throwing up her hands—earning her quite a few strange looks from the hunter guards standing near the entryway to Cavell, though well back away from her. She had figured there would be guards at every entrance to the community but Therin had assigned an additional few to keep an eye on her to ensure she didn't attempt anything untoward.

She blew out a breath, casting a wistful glance up the mouth of the canyon toward the wide open scorching desert.

Was it too late to simply run away? Gods, but she was so badly tempted to do so. She could just leave and never come back. How would they ever even attempt to find her?

But then she frowned in helpless annoyance. With no horse, weapons, or supplies, *and* her luck, if the dragons didn't eat her first, she would probably die of exposure.

Plus, the one thing Oermilla had very successfully drilled into her was that portals weren't the most stable elements of magic. Soleia knew this would make it even bigger of a risk if Callan were to attempt summoning them himself using Dathon's blood. Not only would he be endangering Dathon's life, but Callan would also be endangering his own.

Soleia gritted her teeth. She had to make it work. She had to.

A burst of laughter interrupted her thoughts and she turned toward the community again—a vibrant vision across the dry, brown gorge.

Therin's boisterous, booming laughter mingled with the others' at one of the tables. A citizen passed him a tray of bread and he helped himself.

Soleia couldn't hear but it appeared he was telling stories of the hunt while his audience eagerly leaned in to listen. She pursed her lips. She supposed she couldn't really blame him for his actions.

Therin was deeply respected among his people. And despite his brutality, he was just ensuring their survival. They were hunters. Dragons were game. The desert community knew nothing else. And as Callan had said, times were desperate.

Soleia glanced over at the team of horses still loitering about the cave entryway. Some of them were still heaped with supplies needing to be put away. A handful of hunters and citizens were bustling to task, including Callan and Dathon.

Satisfied with Dathon's impotence, Callan had enlisted his help to unload the loot, and despite his own dislike for Callan, and much to Soleia's astonishment, Dathon had obliged.

Dathon stretched out his arm to receive a complement of tools from one horse to pass them on to another hunter. Only a faint scar remained across his arm on his otherwise already-healed-despite-how-recent injury.

It was honestly incredible.

Soleia could well understand Therin's consternation with not having full access to the monstrous creature with over a hundred times worth of this magical blood.

Unloading an entire season's supplies was strenuous work but it was ironically well suited to Dathon with his innate strength and warrior build. He led one horse back toward the stalls before approaching the next horse to unload. Strands of his hair had worked loose from his tie-back, falling into his eyes as he bent to pick up a wooden crate.

Soleia couldn't help but watch with appreciation as his trousers hugged his hips, the way the muscles on his arms and shoulders flexed as he lifted and turned, those strong fingers grasping the edges of the crate before he passed it along...

Dathon straightened up just then, cracking his neck in strain, and happened to meet her gaze.

Her cheeks warming, Soleia looked away abruptly, shaking off the odd, annoying, thrilling sensations.

He was an evil dragon. He wanted to kill every arrogant Fae he came across. He wanted to kill *her*.

You tricky Fae and your irresponsible use of magic. Are you going to bleed me dry too? You don't even know who I am!

The notion caused a constriction in her chest. She had never really bothered to ask again. And neither Caelina nor her grandmother had a chance to tell her how Dathon had really ended up cursed to the tree or what he had actually done.

Was it possible that he had been misunderstood? What if he was as innocent as he'd claimed? As well as despite his multiple attempts to escape and more than multiple threats to murder her, she couldn't deny that he hadn't really hurt anyone.

Yet.

Although, that probably simply attested to the effectiveness of the curse beads.

Soleia shook her head again to clear the confusion. Regardless. That he was a dangerous creature there was no doubt about and she had certainly already seen how well dragons fought. They would have no qualms about killing, no matter their cause.

A shiver rushed through her upon recalling Dathon's attention when she was cold in the desert, or how he had saved her that last mouthful of water, or the determination with which he'd fought off the prowlers in the desert the other night.

To protect her.

To protect himself?

Ugh. She had to stop thinking about Dathon. Especially when everything relied on her stupid magic that wasn't even working yet.

Just as the last drops of dragon blood on her fingers dissolved into the ether, she rubbed her face with her hands. She had severely underestimated how much she would need. That or she was simply and truly too pathetic to accomplish anything even with the most potent magical blood in the land.

She straightened up with a self-deprecating huff to take a break, marching past the market, past the team of horses. Soleia entered the large communal cavern, heading over to a table with trays of crusty bread beside several water jugs to quell the complaint in her stomach.

Naz and a couple of other hunters were sitting nearby. As soon as she walked past them, the hairs on the back of Soleia's neck stood up, feeling an appraising stare.

Except the hunter wasn't content to just stare.

"Don't do it," Naz called out her warning but the hulking hunter already had a grin on his face as he approached Soleia.

"You're looking mighty frustrated," he noted, clamping one hand on her arm. "How's about we work off some of those pent-up urges?" Then he leaned closer to her face. "I bet I could make even your frigid blood rush to places you've probably forgotten you had."

Her lips curling in distaste, Soleia rolled her eyes.

Before anyone could say anything, she grabbed the hand on her upper arm and whooped him, swinging him by his arm to slam him to the ground on his back with a thud and a small cloud of dust.

Then she stuck the toe of her boot in his throat. "How's about instead I work off this pent-up urge I have to smash in your face?"

Naz and the hunters at her table burst out laughing, fists slamming on the table in mirth.

Callan and Dathon hurried to the entrance of the cavern in alert at the ruckus but the scene was explanation enough. Callan chuckled behind his hand as someone else from the table dragged the hulk back up to his feet.

Soleia beamed the hulk a dry smirk as he brushed himself off and walked back to slump at the table. Wordless. Defeated.

Callan thumped on Dathon's chest with the back of his hand to remark. "Nope. She's not weak."

Soleia's gaze snapped up to them, her eyes narrowing in curiosity. What were they just talking about?

But Callan's shoulders merely shook with humor again before he spun around to get back to work.

Dathon was watching her with a half-smile on his mouth and his eyebrows rose upon noting her walking up to him. His grin widened with his tease. "Some itch I can scratch for you, Princess?"

She gave him a flat look. "You wish." Then she fidgeted in her stance. "I uh... I think I need more blood."

His grin faded and he looked away, shaking his head.

She chewed her bottom lip but beckoned him over. "Callan's workshop is this way."

I4

෨෧

Bloody Truths

Soleia led Dathon through one of the narrow passageways from the main cavern and into a small hollowed-out room. Callan's workshop was furnished with a long wooden table heaped with jars, bowls, and tools, and rudimentary shelving precariously nailed to the walls, holding packs of neatly labeled spices and bottles of ingredients for potions.

She paused for a moment upon coming in as a whiff of cypress tickled her nose. One of Callan's bottles or jars must contain its essence. Soleia couldn't help the memories that the smell brought back.

Fresh, like pine, like the forest. Like home.

Like the once upon a time during her childhood when she and Callan would sneak herbs and potions out of Oermilla's stash to try to summon water spirits from the nearby lake at dusk but instead they would end up scaring each other and then running back to their homes. That had been before she'd found out her magical abilities had stunted. A time when her having magic was a given, when everything still seemed possible.

Dathon had situated himself by the table, and as though it was something he was used to doing, he'd already propped his palm upturned and was folding his sleeve up so she could help herself. He tilted his head, regarding her faraway look. "What is it?"

Despite everything, a smile came to her face. "Nothing. I guess...I just can't believe I'm practicing magic again. I thought I would never—I had stopped hoping. Your blood is truly amazing." She couldn't keep the marvel out of her voice.

Dathon didn't seem as entertained by the notion but she wasn't deterred.

"We were told, of course, of the legend that dragon's blood contained mystical properties," Soleia relayed as she prepared a small blade. "But I had no idea there was a use for everything else too. They really know how not to waste things here in the desert, don't they?"

She shrugged. "It sounds grotesque. I mean, I'm not entirely sure how I feel about it either—and don't get me wrong, dragons are indeed magnificent creatures. But to a hunter, a creature is just a creature. Some they hunt as necessary for their survival." Her eyes widened in wonder. "Aletha tells me dragon's teeth make the best needles and spear tips, and that their early hunters made a kind of delicacy out of certain innards—"

Dathon rolled his eyes, mocking dryly, "Yes, yes, and liver goes well in a stew."

She smirked, going on. "Aletha has the most beautiful

necklace made of dragon scales, but I can imagine scales would also make fantastic armor!" Then she shook her head after a pause. "And then, of course, there's your heart..."

Soleia could barely wrap her head around the possibilities. As if one drop of blood could heal injuries, what wondrous things a clever mind might conceive to concoct from a dragon's heart. It could very well change the world.

But Dathon shot her a look with a catch in it and only spoke after a moment, "You want my heart?"

Her gaze snapped up to meet his, the timbre of his voice and that half-smile on his mouth again shooting a shiver up her spine. She willed her own heart to slow down and pursed her lips, grounding herself back in the reality of the situation. "I want the heart of the dragon," she corrected, matter-of-factly.

He grinned. "Take off these beads and I'll show you."

She met his challenging gaze but then moved to make the small cut, eliciting a momentary cringe from him and he turned his head away. As she carefully collected the blood, her attention distracted to the curse beads around his neck.

You don't even know who I am! How do you know not you're in the wrong here?

She furrowed her eyebrows in pondering. Oermilla had cursed an evil demon. Did Oma and Caelina even know what he was? Not a few days ago, Soleia would have dismissed the doubt immediately as she would have been confident that her sister and grandmother would have certainly told her if dragons were indeed real creatures.

It made her uneasy to think that she now had suspicions about her own family. If they hid the mere fact of his existence, perhaps the reason for his having been cursed was not all that she had been led to believe either.

Soleia forcibly blinked her thoughts away, concentrating on finishing up her task, but she couldn't help her overwhelming curiosity. She cleared her throat, the lump in it making it a chore. "Tell me why you were trapped on that tree. Back in Ipera."

As she'd expected, his entire form stiffened in an instant. Dathon tried to pull away but she held his arm fast, her eyes meeting the storm brewing in his without even flinching. "The truth?" she coaxed before loosening her grip. "Please."

His glare was sharp enough to cut but he seemed to be measuring her tone, the look on her face. Soleia almost thought he was going to shove her away and walk out. But when he realized his death stare didn't work on her, he averted his gaze, huffing in displeasure.

"What I mentioned it before, back at your village. It was half-true," he began almost under his breath. "My people...we are protectors to this land. Dragons keep all magic pure, true, flowing."

Her jaw having dropped in utter disbelief, Soleia took a serious moment to consider if she was simply hearing things. She regarded him with a suspicious look in case he was going to roar with laughter and say it was all a joke again.

But there was no sneering grin this time, no glint in his eyes, no teasing in his tone.

She opened and closed her mouth several times to comment but she couldn't form words, anything coherent anyway.

His eyes darkened at the apparent skepticism on her face.

"See, I knew you wouldn't believe me," he grunted, pushing away to leave.

"Wait." She shook her head. "It's just—this is all very strange and shocking and..." She furrowed her eyebrows as a vague recollection occurred to her. "Oma said the magic of the land is dying."

Dathon didn't turn around. "She's not wrong. Would you like to know why?"

"*You* know why?" She couldn't hide her surprise.

Glancing over his shoulder at her, Dathon pressed his lips in a thin line, his tone grave. "About fifty years ago, an arrogant portal summoner erected boundaries between the realms of Arcadia."

Soleia sucked a breath in, already with a dreaded recognition of where the conversation was heading.

"Except instead of simply protecting certain realms, these spheres of protection disturbed the flow of magic across the land." Dathon's face darkened further. "Meanwhile, some creatures have been trapped within realms to which they do not belong. And for this, they have been hunted down and turned into necklaces and needles."

She shivered as the full impact of his chilling words gripped her.

Therin had wanted to peddle off Dathon's parts for gold. His people would have immediately bled him dry if not for her intrusion. These hunters had been stalking these majestic creatures for decades, creatures who should never have been in the Outlands, to begin with.

She was harvesting his blood to unlock her magic. Her eyes trailed over the multiple faint scars across his exposed arm. She recalled the ones on his back and shoulders, her stomach turning in revolt.

No wonder he hated her. No wonder he hated Fae. No wonder he hated everyone.

"As long as the spheres divide the land, the magic will stagnate and eventually die," Dathon went on. "And as long as my kind is trapped in this realm, we are not safe. These hunters only see me as a prize, a commodity. They rationalize their hunt as this. They all look upon us as evil monsters to be caught, to be feared." His eyes flickered again as they met hers. "As do you."

Soleia's chest heavy with sympathy and remorse, she let out a shaky breath. "I-I'm so sorry, Dathon. I didn't know that." Her eyebrows furrowed as a deep searing tightened in her chest.

With an overwhelming urge to comfort him, she reached out to touch his arm. Finding his skin warm underneath hers, she couldn't help trailing her fingers down, past his wrist, to his fist clenched at his side. She skimmed her fingertips over the scars across his knuckles.

Dathon's eyes cast down, watching her fingers stroke the back of his hand. "Me too...I suppose." He angled to face her. His fist opening, he let his fingers brush between hers.

Soleia's whole arm tingled. Her heart began to pound in her chest. "You too? Are what?"

His gaze darted around. "I never gave you a chance to—I assumed you were only a threat. A typical, heartless Fae. I've been trying to kill you for days. I'm... I'm..." He trailed off.

Soleia's eyebrows rose, only then realizing what he was

trying to say, and she dropped her hand in astonishment. Despite everything, she would have never imagined the evil demon would ever apologize to her. "You...are...what?"

"I'm—"

"Yes?" She blinked at him in expectation.

He threw up his hands with an exasperated groan, moving away. "You are so annoying!"

Watching the protest still flickering in his face, Soleia bit her lip. She watched him pace the floor, her mood lightening somewhat by his hesitation. Not to mention Callan's workshop wasn't so big, it was a sight to see Dathon's large figure try to skulk around it.

But when Dathon met her gaze again, the bemusement on his own face resolved into sobriety, like he wanted her to know he was serious.

He spoke, his voice low. "I'm—sorry." He winced as though he was unused to saying the word. "You are...different." He took another deep breath. "And I don't want you to fear me."

She nodded. "Okay."

His eyes narrowed. "Good."

She couldn't help an amused smile, but when Dathon's gold-red eyes intensified upon her, her heart thumped in her chest again—as though it recognized that this implied the opening up of certain...options.

From the look on his face, Dathon sensed it too.

The silence that followed almost gave Soleia chills again and she swallowed hard. Almost frozen in overwhelm, she blinked hard to snap out of it. "Uhh...I should probably get back to practicing—" she choked out, gesturing to the doorway.

Dathon took a step.

Soleia thought he was moving to leave as well but instead, he walked into her, making her step backward, and then again, until she was flush against the side of the cave.

He pinned her back with nothing more than a look. She let out a slow breath as his mere searing gaze devoured her from head to toe, his eyes traveling down her face, to her mouth, her throat, and then lower, and then there went that sexy, low growl again.

It stirred everything Soleia had been tamping down. Her every nerve ending was alert and awake and hypersensitive to his every breath, to his every subtle movement.

Dathon leaned closer, bracing one hand beside her head, his hair brushing her cheek as he took in her scent. Her name spoken against her neck caused a shiver to run through her. "Soleia..."

The way he said her name had an almost implied possessive.

She gasped at the slightest brush of his lips against the soft skin of her neck, her eyes closing as a crackle of energy rocketed through her.

With no further hint of reservation, Dathon flicked his tongue near her ear, tracing her earlobe, making her insides catch fire and she squirmed against the wall.

His chuckle rumbled in his chest at her encouraging response, his voice still husky. "And that's just my tongue in your ear."

Her sensibilities triggering in raging protest, her eyes flew wide open. *Oh, dear god.* She tried to twist away but he pressed against her and his chest was a solid wall, a light push wasn't going to do it. She heaved against him, glimpsing that cocky grin on his face again.

"I already know you want me," he rasped, pulling back ever so slightly to study her flushed face before his gaze dropped to her mouth again. "And I've wanted to taste those lips since Ipera."

Almost feeling the rest of the world fall away, Soleia swallowed hard between heaves, unable to look away from the blaze in his eyes. He wasn't wrong. She had felt that pull since possibly even long before he'd helped save her village. Butterflies battled in her stomach in anticipation. She licked her lips.

The sight of the tip of her tongue made him groan again but he didn't move an inch. "Say yes." His eyes bore into hers. "Say yes to me."

She could feel his heat through his clothes as she was sure he could feel hers. He was so close, his scent, his face, his mouth...so close...

"Soleia!" Callan called from outside the workshop.

In an absolute startle, Soleia sucked in and flicked her palms out almost instinctively, casting an invisible force making Dathon stagger backward three whole paces.

Soleia's jaw dropped to the floor. *What the—?*

Dathon looked as surprised as she was.

Callan strode into the little cavern. His eyebrows rose in question as Soleia and Dathon were both just standing at either side of the room and staring. "What's...going on here?"

His presence tugged Soleia back into the present. "N-Nothing."

"Therin wants you at the tent," Callan went on, still eyeing the two of them warily.

Soleia straightened up and hurried to exit the workshop first while Callan followed suit. She glanced back, entirely relieved to see that Dathon had enough sense not to pursue them.

Callan's forehead creased at her check. He touched her arm in concern. "What happened? Did he hurt you?"

"No."

He noted her red cheeks. "Is there something going on between you and that beast? I thought you would have been promised to a son of Tarik?"

"I am!" Soleia dismissed, her irritability more from frustration and confusion. "He's an evil dragon. I'm so not going there."

But boy, did she ever want to. She wanted to kick herself in the head. *Ugh!* What the hell even was wrong with her?

"He was just..." She pursed her lips, guilt churning in her stomach again. "Dathon...he said that Great-aunt Helene summoned some barriers across Arcadia and that it's preventing the flow of magic, trapping some creatures from their proper realms."

Callan's eyes clouded as he paused in mid-stride. "I fear you trust far too easily."

Soleia narrowed her eyes at him in disquiet. Was she really so gullible? So easily manipulated? Then again, she had been kept a child in Ipera, with her own family not even revealing to her what threats existed within the realm itself, nor the true nature of the frailty of their world.

Callan gave her a meaningful look. "I suppose he skipped over the reason why Helene felt she had to do that?"

An instant dread crept across Soleia's chest, belatedly realizing Dathon never actually answered her real question. Whether he had done it to divert her on purpose or not, it had worked. She had been too shocked by his revelations to pursue anything else further. "To...to protect people?"

Callan's eyebrows rose. "From what, do you think?" And with nothing more but a pointed shrug, he turned and kept walking.

Soleia took another deep breath, her mind whirling with an overload of scandalizing information. Not in the least of which was that she had let herself get much too vulnerable around the evil dragon. Her face burned hotter even as she hurried to follow Callan.

But putting more distance between her and the cave was helping to clear away the fog in her brain. Soleia struggled to believe that Helene had erected these powerful barriers dividing the land on a mere whim, thereby causing all these problems. She had to believe that Helene must have had a very solid, very reasonable, very necessary reason to do so.

That meant Dathon must have been lying again, right?

Right?

Soleia shook her head to dismiss her confusion. *Dammit all.* This debate was ridiculous and absolutely ill-timed. She needed to focus. Whatever Helene or Dathon did or didn't do was irrelevant for the moment. Helene was gone. And Soleia would deal with the dragon later.

The hunters were moving ahead with their plans.

15

Far Too Easily

Soleia ducked under the lowered canvas flaps to come into the briefing tent. Therin and half a dozen of his hunters were crowded around the table of maps, the worn paper scrolls lit bright orange by the late afternoon sun reflecting against the tarp above their heads.

Callan met her by the entryway and she smiled at him. He handed her a goblet of drink before beckoning her to come closer to the table.

Therin was going through the evening's plan of attack, through all the information they had collected from the scouts so far—the den's vantage points, sentry change schedules, potential weak points for possible ingress.

Soleia met Therin's cutting gaze over the rim of her goblet as she took a sip, his next statement seeming to be directed at her.

"In case it warrants repeating," he said, "the dragon's den

is built on a canyon ridge with the top of the structure being a large open cavern, making it easy for the dragons to fly in and out. But it has always been too steep of a climb from the desert floor. The desert surrounds also have a sentry or two posted round the clock. That's in addition to the lookouts at the top of the towers since every time we come within even a thousand yards of the den, we've already been spotted."

Soleia's eyes narrowing, she couldn't help but remark, "This sounds like a suicide mission."

Therin grunted before meeting Soleia's eye. "I am risking my people with you so it better not be." His displeasure was clear but what was even clearer to Soleia was that an undertaking such as this would have been impossible indeed without either the assistance of a dragon itself or a means to enter the impregnable fortress stealthily—such as, oh say, portals.

Today truly was Therin's lucky day.

He raised his voice again. "Three teams. I will lead the first. Naz will lead the second. Take Otto, the girl, the dragon, and no more than two others through the portal to secure the sentries to make way for us. Callan and the others with the gift will follow as reinforcements."

He jerked his thumb back toward the giant hunter. "Hill will stay behind with Callan to make sure we get what we need from the dragon—that is in case you fail to generate a portal." His eyes flashed at Soleia once more. "So I hope you've reined in that power of yours, little mage."

Little mage... Soleia's stomach churned. Not wanting to expose her apprehension, she gave him a cool glare and sneered, "So inspiring."

In an attempt to quell her frayed nerves, instead, she

relegated her thoughts to blind optimism. And after the near involuntary blast at Callan's workshop, she was even almost hopeful. She was close. She had to be.

Assuming she did manage to control her magic, perhaps she could portal straight back to Ipera. She could hail a sandstorm to wallop all the hunters across the desert, then portal home just to check on Caelina, and then finally portal away to the human realm. She might even still have a chance to be free as she had initially planned. Her heart pounded at the possibilities but she willed her expression to stay neutral.

Therin merely grunted. He turned back toward the map, flicking a point on the scroll with his fingers, giving it a loud clack. "Time it right, you should be able to subdue the sentries so my team can ride in to engage the dragons and lead them away," he was telling Naz. "Meanwhile, you locate the treasure, pack up the loot, and scale down on the rig to escape." He gestured to a pile of ropes in the corner.

Therin's tone was all business. Soleia noted the focused expressions of every one of the hunters as they listened intently. None of them showed any foreboding about the plan whatsoever. None of them seemed hesitant or nervous. They obviously had great trust in Therin.

"Given nobody screws up, we should be back at Cavell by sun up with the loot—including this rumored all-powerful artifact." Therin dusted off his hands as if in ceremonial conclusion. "Is that solid?"

Nods and low murmurs of agreement abound the tent.

Therin gave Soleia an expectant look and she shifted her gaze toward Callan who already had a slight grimace on his face. Callan gave her a short nod as if pleading with her to acquiesce.

The wheels in her head were still spinning. If she summoned a portal, she could take Dathon and maybe even Callan and escape to Ipera. Naz and the others would remain in Cavell. The dragon's den would be left alone. She would be leaving everyone no worse off than they were had she not arrived. No harm done. And since by that time, Therin's team would have already left, he wouldn't have a chance to harm her or Dathon and make good on his murderous threats. He would never be able to coordinate a pursuit.

Except, it all seemed too easy.

Turning to meet Therin's gaze again, Soleia narrowed her eyes. "How do you know I won't just run?"

And the most self-assured grin spread over Therin's face. "Well...if you run, you'll never get this." He reached inside his cloak front and held up a little vial with a yellow liquid.

She squinted. "What is that?"

Therin hid a smile, his eyes flickering toward the goblet in Soleia's hand. "The antidote."

Her face paling, Soleia dropped the goblet, its remaining contents sloshing across the ground. Her eyes lit up in rage. She leaped to pounce at Therin but not before two hunters held her back.

Spitting out the taste in her mouth, Soleia stared at the spill absorbing into the sand before raising her eyes to meet Callan's.

Guilt was written all over his face. "I'm so sorry, Soleia."

Therin chuckled low. "Don't worry yet. It's a particularly

special poison. It shouldn't interfere with your magic. It stays in your system for a few hours, harmless, dormant, until…" He made a retching sound to punctuate his sentence.

Somehow, Soleia broke free from the hunters. She roared as she lunged at Therin again, landing a fist squarely across the old man's face before more hunters went to subdue her. Rage welling up in her chest, Soleia yanked away from one of them, engaging her fists at anything that moved. She had just reached for her dagger when—

"Soleia!" Callan cried out in alarm.

"All of you, stop!" Therin barked his command. He'd staggered back, slightly winded, but he motioned his hunters to stand down with one hand, wiping his mouth with the back of the other.

Soleia stopped her blade's end short of another hunter's face as the brute backed away.

Therin met Soleia's acid gaze evenly. There was no remorse in his cold eyes but no delight either. "You probably think I'm being cruel but I'm putting my people's lives in your hands and I don't exactly trust you. Either way, if you fail, we still have your dragon."

Breathless, Soleia's held her chin stiff. "How much time do I have?"

"Enough," Therin stated before giving her a pointed look. "So instead of spiting me, I would suggest you focus on getting the job done. Then," he proposed with a chilling smile, "perhaps we'll all be happy."

* * *

Soleia was glad that Boots had been kept at the rearmost stall in the farthest cavern. With the hunters preparing for the upcoming mission and the team of horses having come back from this morning's hunt still needing tending, enough people were bustling in and out of the stables to create a constant draft.

There was also enough urgency, tension, and nerves in the air, Soleia didn't want to be in anyone's way. Overhearing several whispered discussions, she had gleaned that the last time they had attempted to breach the den, many of the hunters had not returned.

Aletha was near the entrance along with several other citizens who were helping ready the horses. She had given back Soleia's clothes from yesterday, freshly washed, and Soleia had put them on again. Her new dress, no matter how pretty, was not going to be suitable for a hike up a nearly inaccessible canyon and potential dragon battle.

Although after Soleia thanked her earlier, Aletha had given her a soft smile but hadn't engaged her in conversation. Soleia wondered if she had heard about Therin's poison trick. Not that Soleia would have wanted it advertised.

Then again, there were also good odds that the poison could have even been of Aletha's making. It was a stark reminder that to her, these people were all still, in fact, strangers. Perhaps even enemies.

Soleia squeezed her eyes shut for a moment, remorse stabbing at her heart. She put a hand to her chest, taking two deep breaths as though a guarantee. The poison indeed seemed to be harmless as she felt none of its effects so far.

I'm putting my people's lives in your hands...

Therin was ruthless but he wasn't entirely wrong. He was a desperate man, trying to protect his people amidst desperate times. If the community didn't receive an influx of supplies before the cold weather descended, many of the citizens would not survive.

She only hoped Therin had enough men to undertake their miraculous endeavor, that everything went according to plan, and that the poison stayed dormant for as long as possible. The strain of further extortions had drained all her earlier hope. She had even less time now.

The orange sun streaking through the small stone windows glinted off her sword blades and she ran her fingers down the cool metal almost in pining before hoisting the scabbard harness off of her horse to sling back around her shoulders.

Right away, she felt twice as confident, twice as reassured, and amongst the crowd of strangers in the stables, significantly less alone...

The swinging door to the stables slammed open and grabbed everyone's attention.

Soleia looked up to see Dathon in the doorway. Heaving, his eyebrows were knitted together in urgency, but whatever alarm was in his eyes flickered upon spotting her.

They hadn't spoken since the incident at Callan's workshop. Soleia had decided it didn't matter if he had been telling the truth or not. She still had no business involving herself with the dangerous dragon in the first place, even if he was no longer trying to kill her.

Even if the intensity of his arrival, his mere presence, set her pulse racing.

Dathon made his way toward her, wending around several

citizens, brushing past Aletha's group. His gaze was pinned solely on Soleia so he wouldn't have noticed most of the people steering wide clear of his path as always, nor that one of the more courageous human females he'd passed by had given him a little flirty smile over her shoulder.

Observing that, Soleia's eyebrows shot up her forehead and as Dathon arrived near Boots' stall, she couldn't help but quip, "Oh, look, someone's got a death wish—"

And then she was in his arms.

Her face nestled in the crook of his neck, Soleia blinked in surprise as Dathon's warmth enveloped her.

Aletha had at least the insight to tap the earlier female's shoulder for attention, whispering something to her, glancing back at Soleia and Dathon in turn with a knowing smirk on her lips before gesturing for everyone to focus back to work.

Dathon folded Soleia up against him, tighter as though of some reassurance that she wasn't going to disappear. His fearful words murmured above her head, "I heard about the poison. I-I thought—"

She took a deep breath in realization. Dathon must have thought Therin had gotten too impatient with her magic and perhaps decided it was pointless to keep her alive after all. Despite herself, she couldn't help a little flutter at his concern. She shook her head. "No. Well," she amended. "Yes, sort of, but I'm fine for now."

He pulled back just enough to study her face. His forehead still creased deeply, he looked her up and down. "Are you sure? Are you sick? Are you feeling weak?"

Soleia frowned. She did feel sick. Sick to her stomach. Callan hadn't attempted to speak to her since the tent either but she was almost glad for it. She didn't need his apologies. She could barely stand to look at him. Soleia had lost Callan to the Outlands. She had lost her brother.

"It seems you were right before. Even family can deceive you," she stated.

Seeming compelled to comfort her, or he was looking to pick up where they had left off from Callan's workshop, Dathon steeled his jaw, lifting a hand to tilt her chin up toward him. "Soleia..."

Soleia's skin tingled. His touch conveyed reassurance, security. She looked up to meet the raw concern in his gold-red eyes and it felt as though she had put on her double sword scabbard a dozen times.

He couldn't stop touching her face. He brushed her hair back and stroked her cheek, her chin. His fingers slid past her throat so he could cup the nape of her neck with one hand, unable to help his gaze dropping to her mouth.

But Soleia jerked away when he leaned in. A prickly feeling of vulnerability washed over her and she crossed her arms over her chest as if to ward herself against him. The mention of Callan's betrayal was just a bleak reminder of everything else.

Everyone was lying to her. She was surrounded by deceit.

"And you..." she spoke under her breath. "Callan said Helene put up the barriers to protect everyone *from* dragons." She couldn't mask the bitter protest in her tone. "Why would she protect the land from its own guardians? Unless dragons *are* the threat themselves, ravaging the lands for decades like all the legends say."

Dathon dropped his hand and stepped away altogether. "That wasn't me."

She shot him a look. His withdrawal and change in posture were an instant giveaway, his eyes offended but also guilty.

He glanced away for a moment before his admission. "Yes, certain dragons were wreaking havoc among the realms, playing tricks, possibly setting accidental fires. They weren't supposed to do that." He met her gaze in earnest. "I didn't lie when I said dragons are custodians of Arcadia. But some of these dragons, they've...lived a long, privileged life. And sometimes when they're bored, they..." he trailed off with a shrug.

Soleia gave him an even look. "That sounds suspiciously exactly like you."

He snarled. "It's not!"

The look in his eyes was so indignant and pleading, something tugged at her heart. She wanted to believe him.

Then again if Callan was a traitor, could she really trust anything he told her either? Callan could have been lying about dragons too.

She no longer knew what to believe.

Soleia groaned in frustration. "You know what? That doesn't even matter right now." She cast a wary glance at the other groups of citizens in the stable before lowering her voice. "I've got more important things to worry about. I'm trying to save your life? Among other things?"

Dathon narrowed his eyes. "Therin's using the poison as—"

"Oh, it's definitely a great motivator." Soleia couldn't help but roll her eyes. "He'll only give me the antidote once I form the portal. But I've been trying all day and guess what? No portals. Not a one. Not even half of one. This is ridiculous!" she hissed. "I couldn't fathom summoning portals for twenty-one years. There's no way I was going to grasp it in one day. And it's almost sundown!"

Studying her face, his chin set in determination. Dathon tugged on her arm. "Come with me."

16

❧

Yes

Soleia glanced back in marvel at the cave tunnels they had climbed through and come out of. There was an overhang of a small oasis ensconced within a canyon hollow where scant shrubs grew around a small catchment of water just beneath the trail. It was quite rare being so high up.

She trudged her way toward the edge of the ridge and upon reaching the top, miles and miles of a desert panorama greeted her in every direction. The towering canyons, scattered rock formations, the sands glimmering as the sun dipped low on the horizon. She could almost sight the entire expanse of the Outlands, from the western ranges to the horizon where the sea met land. The gusty wind whipped strands of her hair that had come loose from her braid at her face.

Dathon's crunching steps came from behind her.

Her face aglow with amazement, she turned to him with a smile. "How do you know about this place?"

Surveying the desert, he moved to stand beside her. "Cavell's canyon is full of hidden tunnels which perhaps its citizens aren't even aware exist. But I can hear where the wind slips through, the cracks and crevices it seeks to exit."

Puzzled, she shot him another look. "You could have left," she realized. "Why didn't you escape using the hidden tunnels?" He'd certainly had more than one opportunity to do so and Therin hadn't poisoned *him*.

Dathon didn't shift his gaze. "I told you why."

A pang of guilt streaked her chest as her eyes fell on the curse beads around his neck once again. His real prison. She'd need but remove them and he would be freed.

Soleia pursed her lips, for the first time battling with thoughts of defying Oermilla's instructions, of perhaps actually releasing him...

But she forcibly shook it off.

Different problem for later.

Focus.

She cleared her throat. "So what are we doing here?"

"Your magic needs to breathe." He gestured wide across the plateau. "I'll help you channel it. Summoning that portal will be the fastest way to get you that antidote."

Chewing on her lip, Soleia's gaze darted around. She wasn't sure how a change in scenery could help her hone her magic. Already downcast, she threw up her hands. "I don't know what else I can do. I've tried—everything."

His eyes narrowed. "Is this you giving up? Then we *are* going to die."

"But this magic..."

Turning, he shook his head. "You don't even understand your powers."

She thought he was reaching for her. But he grasped the straps of her scabbard harness and proceeded to slide them off of her. She held in a gasp as Dathon pushed the straps past her shoulders, down her arms. He dropped her swords on the ground with a metallic clank.

"You don't need these."

He was leaning close enough to her that Soleia couldn't help but study the elegant line of his jaw, watch wayward strands of his silver hair whip around his face, his shirt billowing in the wind showing off his chest.

And despite what she had resolved about him, being alone with him again like this still sent shivers up her spine.

His voice was smooth as he circled her slowly, the words spoken near her ear. "Portal summoning is about making what's unseen seen, what's intangible tangible. It's reaching out into the world, making connections... You need to feel what's around you, see through its eyes, hear music in the silence."

Somehow when Oma's exact same words came from Dathon's mouth they had a drastically different effect. She most certainly didn't want to doze off right then. But how could he have possibly known those words?

Unable to help the wariness in her tone, she turned to him. "How do you know so much about this magic?"

"Helene."

Soleia blinked in recognition.

"Nobody was supposed to know about the existence of

my people. That was why only the legends about dragons survived. But Helene...she—" His face darkened at the memory. "She betrayed us."

The hatred and bitterness roiling in his eyes were much like what had been there when Soleia had first found him pinned against the tree in the wraith forest. The mere notion of Helene had set him off then as it did now. The darkness swirled in his eyes, curled his mouth, and barbed his entire countenance.

She watched the memories flicker beneath his eyes until they seemed to catch on something less...loathsome.

"It didn't start that way." Dathon's gaze was far away. "I thought we were friends—I... It was my fault." He shook his head. "Before Helene, no Fae had ever sensed my presence. But she was able to feel into our hidden world, and against my better judgment, I showed myself." Tilting his head, he paused at the recollection. "I guess we surprised each other. But she had promised to keep our secrets, and in return, she told me about the abilities of a portal summoner, and showed me some of your people's sacred and magical places all across the continent."

Soleia studied his wistful expression and almost scoffed in disbelief. "Oh my god, were you in love with my Great-aunt?"

He gave her a wry look. "Do you mean if she hadn't cursed me and left me pinned to a tree for half a century?"

Her eyes lit up as it clicked. "*She* cursed you," she rasped. "That's how you ended up on the tree in the wraith forest."

"Well, she had become adamant that dragons were atrocities, a great threat to the land, a menace, and that she needed to expose us to protect the realms once and for all!" The disquieting frustration was still fresh in his tone. "I tried to reason with her but she wouldn't listen. She was so full of rage. We fought—"

He stopped short, looking away again. "She knew she couldn't kill me so she just... The last thing I remember is...her blade. And a blurry vision of your grandmother."

There was no tremor of hesitation, no trace of pretense on his face. Only a deep-seated sense of anger and regret.

Soleia's stomach churned in mortification. While she'd had a vague idea of the magnitude of Great-aunt Helene's power, she'd never imagined this.

But Dathon took a deep, almost cleansing breath—of one who wished perhaps to finally leave things in the past.

"Helene tore down the veil that hid my people and brought up the spheres. I never thought she would do it— never thought she *could* do it. Only one with such a mastery of that power could have done what she did. Access to that level of magic, reaching all across the land, was unheard of. Her power was...incredible." His tone changed for a moment with somewhat revered awe.

After a somber moment, his gaze settled on her. "But I feel the same power in you, the same strength, the same resilience. You think you are weak because you are unable to access your magic. But you are not weak. You *can* do this."

Desperate exasperation struck her again. "How?"

"Think back," he soothed. "Earlier at Callan's workshop, you were starting to regard your magic fondly once again. So think back to when you first learned magic, what it felt like, what it meant for you."

Soleia rarely willingly looked back to those days. Such

happy days only ended with the memory of her parents' death and the anguish it had caused not just her family but the entire village; a lingering pain that still cut deep, rippling across her soul. Then one by one, everything seemed to tumble away. Her magic disappeared. Her sister got married off. Callan ran away. And she had nothing left.

The ache in her heart deepening, Soleia took a deep breath to shake off all the memories. "Look, I don't see how any of this is going to help. All I can remember is loss." Her tone cracked slightly. "My parents—"

Dathon cut in, quite unconcerned. "My parents died too, you don't see me being all pathetic and useless about it."

The statement stabbed at her chest and she gritted her teeth, but after a moment, she blinked to clear her head. He was provoking her on purpose.

"You're using that as a crutch, an excuse." His tone was stern. "You wish to dwell on what the magic has taken *from* you. You've somehow convinced yourself that you are nothing without the things you have lost. You cannot see how much you have. How much you *are*."

He reached for her hand, lifting it in front of her. Then he slit his palm with the edge of one sharp claw and pressed his hand against hers.

Soleia gazed up into his eyes even as he searched hers. The combination of his words and the essence of his blood were making her light-headed. Tingling crept up her arms, her neck, awakening the magic. Again, there was an easing to that vague aching deep inside her, a culmination, a completion...

Dathon moved to hover behind her once more. His fingers

caressed down her braid, and his other hand slid down to her hip, strong fingers grasping, possessing, holding her still.

Heat flushed right through her from his touch. "I am sure you don't need to be holding on to me like that," she mused.

"And yet I am going to." His breath on the nape of her neck, his voice was husky. "Now find your power. Will it back."

Unable to hide her smile, she inhaled deeply, and then with a shaky release, Soleia closed her eyes. A gentle breeze blew across her face. With the sun dipping down in the sky, the temperature would have dropped a touch. But Dathon's warmth reached out to her and when she relaxed her shoulders, she couldn't help but nestle backward.

Dathon let her melt against him, his jaw brushing the side of her head as he spoke, "See with the desert, hear what it's saying."

Soleia reached out with her mind and the wind answered. It whistled as it seeped through cracks and hollows in the mountain ridge. The heat of the sun sizzled in the air, hissing against the soft sands where burrowing critters chittered underground. Across the continent, she could almost hear the repeated pattering of waves against the shoreline from the great sea.

A sudden sense of being flung too far away and possibly not being able to return almost overwhelmed her, but the firm reminder of Dathon's strength against the line of her back grounded her to the present and reinforced calm over her trance.

Just then, the shadow of great wings flittered across the eyes in her mind and she gasped. She could almost hear the beast screeching as it soared in the dusky sky.

"What do you see?" Dathon murmured in her ear.

An intense warmth surged in her chest as the magic built up inside, carrying with it echoes of vast memories, of whispered secrets, of pasts revealed, of shadowy visions of a future...shrouded in a murky mist.

She couldn't quite wipe the fog away to discern what lay hidden beneath it. But she could almost see it, almost taste it...

The faint thundering of hooves snapped her out of her reverie.

Opening her eyes, Soleia glimpsed a team of horses riding out from Cavell headed toward the next ridge.

Therin's hunters had ridden out.

She darted an alarmed glance toward the mountains across the desert. The sun had set, painting the sky a dark fuchsia hue.

Her chest clenched tight in distress and she lost all grip on the magic. "We're out of time." Whirling around, she let out a loud frustrated yell. "I can't make it work!"

"You were almost there. I could feel it. Try again," Dathon urged.

Blowing out a breath, Soleia squeezed her eyes shut once more and tried to concentrate but the noise in her head grew unbearable.

Sundown. It was sundown. It was too late. She couldn't do it. She was going to die. The poison was going to take her. Therin would bleed Dathon dry. Callan would fall to the unstable magic.

Her knees shaking, she almost couldn't stay upright.

Raging protest bubbled up in her chest. Why was this even happening to her? If she had never run away, she would have never unleashed the cursed dragon. If she had just risked humiliation back at her village, she would have never fallen into the hunters' trap. Why hadn't she just listened to her sister? Where was the nobler-than-thou Caelina who could take over everything and do it perfectly? Soleia was the last person in the world who should be expected to handle all this.

Dathon must have noticed the mounting frustration on her face. He snapped, "Don't give in to your fears. Stop rejecting your power. It's part of you. You have to own it. Surrender to it, Soleia."

Her eyes flying open, she let out another cry. "I can't!"

Dathon tried to reach for her but she raised her arms and snapped her hands down with a yell, "I said I can't!"

A sharp gust of wind made him stagger back, nearly teetering off the rim of the plateau and he gaped down at his feet as he warily stepped away from the ledge. "Did you just— repel me?" He shot her a look of disbelief.

Trying to stop from heaving, she bit her lip. "I—I wasn't trying to—"

With a challenging look in his eyes, he cocked his head, his demeanor shifting instantly. "Ohhh...so you want to play? I suppose I could do with a little distraction."

"Whoa." She held up her hand for him to stop, her squeal trapped in her throat. "Whoa, hey! We really don't have time for this."

His eyes flashed. "You started it."

"Dathon, don't—" Soleia's eyes widened in dread but in

spite of herself, she broke away running. He tried to lunge for her and she raised her hands again to repel him but he kicked off the ground, leaping at her again.

"Hey—" Soleia tucked and rolled on the ground out of the way.

Dathon grinned as he straightened up. "You're still pretty nimble."

Exasperated, she tilted her head. "And you're still really cocky."

"Oh, you have no idea."

Soleia's eyes drifted toward her swords on the ground but when she dove to grab a sword, he grabbed the other one before she could. He met her gaze with a sly grin, gripping the sword to level before him.

Holding her blade to one side, Soleia got into a stance. She threw her shoulders back airily, her tension having dissipated. "This was a bad move, Curse Boy." She shook her head ruefully. "Need I remind you of the last time you tried to challenge me and I kicked your ass up and down the desert?"

He pursed his lips. "Oh, which time? That time when you were cheating?" He lunged forward with the sword but Soleia parried easily. She swished his blade away with a snap of her wrist and quick-stepped sideways to avoid his counter.

Dathon thrust left and right and she swung to block twice.

Breathless, she interjected, "I could just say the binding word and all this will be over in a second."

He countered and parried. "Sure, but that would be you admitting—*again*—that you really can't beat me with your own merits." He winked at her but Soleia hissed at him. She didn't want him to be right either.

Dathon shot forward, sliding on the coarse ground on his knees to strike to her left but she jumped clear of him and whipped around to block his strike.

Clashing metal to metal echoed within the canyon hollow, the scratching and scraping of loose rocks and gravel grinding underfoot, grunts and shouts of strain, of frustration, of hits and misses, amidst the squall of the fading light.

Another few swift strikes and counters and Soleia feinted, swatting the sword right out of Dathon's grasp. Her eyes lighting up in victory, she watched the blade slide sideways across the flat. "Hah!"

And when Soleia thrust forward with her sword once more, Dathon leaped backward but it seemed he'd underestimated the space left. His eyes bulged as he leaned precariously too close to the edge of the plateau again.

"Watch the ledge!" Soleia dropped her sword with a clatter. She grasped his outstretched hand before he could slip and tugged him toward her. But with his face inches away from hers, she glimpsed his superior grin.

He had planned for that.

Without warning, he pushed off, disrupting her balance, and he spun them around so that instead she was teetering back by the rim of the canyon with nothing but his grip on her arm holding her up.

His eyes gleaming, Dathon noted, "See, I can cheat too."

Wide-eyed, Soleia glanced over her shoulder at the hundred-foot drop as stones and chunks of red soil beneath her feet crumbled down the ledge and when he met her gaze again, hers was sincerely murderous. "You are so annoying."

Dathon chuckled, giving her another sharp tug, and

whether he'd meant to or not, he tumbled back, taking Soleia with him right into a tackle as he flipped over to pin her down.

He met her sharp gaze. "Surrender."

Still heaving, Soleia rolled her eyes in bemusement and annoyance as she tried to push him off with a grunt to no avail.

Dathon gazed down at her in triumph, his focus dropping to her mouth for a moment. "Surrender," he said again.

She pressed her lips together before meeting his gaze evenly, pointedly. "No."

Dathon winced, almost already in expectation of the blinding pain from the binding spell.

Except nothing happened.

He blinked, meeting her gaze again.

Soleia looked just as shocked—but then it clicked.

You have to mean it strongly.

Dathon's eyes widened at the realization, the relief and pleasure reflecting on his face. Save for the whistling wind gusting across the desert, there was only silence as he studied her face in his shadow.

Soleia couldn't tear her eyes away from his. Incredibly terrified, but at the same time, exhilarated, there was no calming her heart down and she realized his heartbeat was pounding in his chest as well.

Dathon had done it. He had broken through her resolve.

Had he swayed her convictions? Had he actually earned her trust? Did she no longer deem him a threat? Had he finally overcome her defenses?

One corner of Dathon's mouth turned up as he bent his head low, murmuring, "Yes..." His long fingers plunged into her hair, curling firm around her head, making chills shoot through her entire being. Soleia's eyes closed of their own accord such that she almost missed the sudden glow of flickering light.

And before Dathon's lips could land on hers, the rocky ground gave way beneath her.

"Whoa—"

The next second, the two of them fell to the floor right at Boots' feet at his stall.

The stables had emptied except for a couple of citizens who were brushing the thoroughbred. But when Soleia and Dathon dropped in from nowhere, the women squealed in surprise, immediately dropping their brushes before scurrying toward the cavern exits.

Sitting up on the matted hay, Soleia blinked in shock.

Equally stunned, Dathon jumped up to standing. "Was that—?"

"Did I just—"

When he turned back to her, his smile was nearly blinding. "You just did. You did it."

Soleia's chest felt as though it was about to burst.

She did it. She finally did it.

Then her face fell. "Ah, dammit, my swords." Someone was going to have to go back up to the ridge to collect them. Except for the first time, she didn't feel quite so unnerved, didn't feel as though she was missing an appendage.

She reached up to grab Dathon's outstretched hand. But

when he pulled her up, he caught her in an embrace once more, his words laced with elation and amazement rumbling deep in his chest.

"You...are...magnificent."

Mesmerized by the sudden tenderness in his brilliant gold-red eyes as he gazed down at her, Soleia couldn't help smiling again.

A terse voice by the door dragged her back down to the present.

"It's time," Naz barked.

17

Portal

"*Hya!*" Soleia kicked the horse into a gallop, riding out into the desert.

The wind swirling around her, whipping past Boots, Soleia closed her eyes and took a deep breath. She made it about a hundred yards out from the canyon entrance but—

Still no portal.

She opened her eyes, slowing down before leading Boots to turn around. In complete exasperation and annoyance, she tipped what remained of the newly-extracted dragon blood from the vial onto her hands all at once before kicking off to ride back toward Cavell again.

At her command, Boots sped off once more. Soleia squeezed her eyes shut, concentrating on the energy tingling up her arms from the dragon blood and—

Still no portal.

With a groan of frustration, Soleia pulled on Boots' reins

to screech to a stop just before Naz's bored posture. Naz's elbow was slung over Otto's shoulder. "What are you doing?"

Panting, Soleia made a face. The magic was draining her fast. "I'm—trying to recreate the portal—from the first time I used it to leave Ipera."

"Well, it's clearly not working. We're wasting time!" Naz wailed out loud.

The second team of horses standing by with Callan and his hunters, all suited up and ready, were waiting at the mouth of the gorge. They were meant to ride out as soon as Soleia formed the portal to the den.

Not to mention the handful of Cavell citizens standing by, including Aletha, who was also watching, curiosity piqued at the prospect of witnessing a portal summoner possibly for the first and only time in their lives. It would have been nothing short of a miracle.

Except—there was still no portal.

"Six attempts by my count," Otto quipped, looking bored.

Flanked by two more giant hunters to one side, Hill had Dathon's arm gripped tight. "Can we just gut the dragon already?" Hill drawled.

From atop Boots, Soleia glanced over to meet Callan's anguished face. It looked like he wanted to say something in her defense but she slid her gaze away toward Dathon instead. Her posture haggard, she rasped, "I'm...I'm so sorry—"

Dathon's eyebrows were already snapped together in concern and he tried to shove Hill away. "Let me go to her."

Hill, whose grip had initially tightened, acknowledged Naz's nod at him to let the dragon go.

Dathon rushed forward and helped Soleia to dismount.

She nearly collapsed in his arms. "I can't do it, Dathon. This is all my fault. I should have listened to you. We should have just left right away."

He shook his head, steeling his jaw. "That doesn't matter. Right now, you need to portal us to the den one time so we can finish this quickly and get you the antidote from Therin. It's the only way."

"It's too hard. I don't even know where to go."

His forehead creased and he cradled her face in his hand. "Perhaps I can show you," he soothed. "The best spot to portal is the top of the ridge. There's a lookout point that's mostly hidden from the courtyard. From there, it will be easier for Naz to spot the tower sentries and for Otto and the others to disarm the ground sentries from above."

Soleia blinked in surprise. "But how will you—?"

"Dragons can communicate by thought," Dathon reminded her. "I can try to make you see with my eyes."

Hill was tapping a dagger against a metal cufflink on his arm. "Can we *please* gut the dragon already so we can all get going?" He looked to Naz for approval and when she finally gave him another short nod, Hill advanced on Dathon and yanked on his arm.

"Hey—!" Dathon growled even as he staggered backward.

Soleia's chest squeezed in helplessness. "Wait!" she insisted, putting her hand up. "Please. Let me just catch my breath. I have—another idea."

Naz's frown was getting sterner by the moment. But she looked to Callan whose face was pale, distraught, and her expression wavered. Letting out a short groan, she bid a short wave. "*One* last chance, mage."

Her stomach churning, Soleia nodded fervently. Moving toward Boots, she stroked his mane. "I need to do something, boy," she whispered as she walked the horse to one side. "Stay here with Callan. But if he tries anything, feel free to kick him in the head."

Then she cast Hill a pointed look, gesturing to his captive. "I'll need him back."

Hill grunted as he shoved Dathon away once more.

Soleia held out her hand to him which he took and she pulled him toward her. She had one last chance. She only needed to summon a proper portal *once*.

She gave Dathon's questioning look an unamused but dry glare. "Indulge me." She grabbed his shirtfront and tugged him even closer.

Dathon's eyes widened, a hint of a smirk playing on his lips as he cast a glance around at everyone staring but he didn't move and let her lead.

"What the hell is she playing at now?" Naz looked aggravated.

Callan's eyebrows merely shot up his forehead as he watched.

Portals were such tricky, annoying elements of magic. If Soleia'd had the opportunity to mentor with Helene, she would have at least been familiar with its particular quirks. But as fate would have it, she was going to have to figure it out as she went along.

That was if extracted dragon blood was insufficient to sustain the magic required perhaps she had to go right to the source.

Drawing her dagger from her thigh, Soleia instructed, "Give me your palm."

Dathon obliged and she slit his hand as he had done himself back on the ridge.

When Soleia clasped her palm in his, she gasped as the potent force of the magic surged through her again. His blood pulsed against her skin with a direct connection to his beating heart. She took a deep breath and stared up into his eyes. "Alright, show me where to go."

Unable to hide a fascinated smile, Dathon leaned forward, bracing his forehead against hers, and the same warmth and reassurance flowed through her. With her breathing loud in her ears, she let her eyes flutter closed, swept away her thoughts, and opened her mind to touch Dathon's.

The suddenness of the visions almost jolted her.

Flashes of a brightly lit landscape funneled into her mind. The canyon ridge. The large open courtyard. The sun whipped across the sky, colors changing from yellow to orange to violet. A blanket of stars. A rock face. A boulder in the shadows. And even with her lids shut, Soleia could sense a growing brightness from underneath her.

His face close to hers, Soleia felt Dathon whisper the awed words near her mouth. "It's working."

She tipped her chin up, her lips almost brushing against his. "Yes…"

Her eyes flew open when the sand beneath them gave way and they fell feet first through the portal before tumbling back on an uneven surface.

Soleia's head shot up to survey their surroundings, almost

already in distress over whatever threat their new surroundings posed.

Dathon pushed up off the rocky ground beside her and met her gaze.

Did it work?

From behind a large boulder, Soleia glimpsed a wide stone plateau beneath them that seemed to have been carved out of the side of the mountain. The sky was turning shades of dark purple making it difficult to make out what was below but just then a large dark shadow whooshed above their heads.

Soleia's heart pounded in her chest as she edged back in her seat to ensure she was not seen by the creature looking to make a landing in the middle of the courtyard.

Scales gleaming in the moonlight, red beady eyes, its snout still steaming, the dragon poofed into a dark cloud before a figure of a man emerged as the creature shifted. The man ambled his way into a crevice off to one side to head into the den.

They were definitely not in Cavell anymore.

It had worked.

And the surprise seemed effective as their arrival had not raised any alarms that she could notice. Dathon had picked the perfect spot on the lookout as the huge boulder hid any trace of them from a clear view of the courtyard or any of the lookout towers. The sentries hadn't been alerted nor were they particularly on guard.

Straightening up, she met Dathon's awed gaze and he gave her a half-smile before reaching down to take her hand and squeezing it.

She almost burst in relief and pride but then her knees trembled in her stance for a moment, feeling a bit winded. It was either Therin's poison finally seeping through her veins or the full realization that they were finally at the dragon's den. The most dangerous place in the Outlands.

When she looked up, Dathon's worried eyes were waiting but she gave him a small, dismissive smile. He slipped his fingers between hers and instead of a paralyzing fear of what they were about to face, a fresh surge of reassurance spread through her.

She was safe. She had summoned the miraculous portal. The hard part was done. She was going to be okay now. Everything was going to be okay now.

Naz, Otto, and two others with the climbing rig fell through the bright, swirling portal. A not-quite-liquid silvery sphere hovered in mid-air behind them, its dazzling light flickering across their faces before it dissipated in the next instant as though nothing had been there at all.

Crouching low, Naz cast a glance over at Soleia and Dathon. If Naz was impressed that Soleia was finally able to summon a portal, she definitely didn't show it. She merely met Soleia's gaze with a short nod.

Soleia nodded in acknowledgment. They had all agreed to silence until the den was secure.

Naz gestured with her arm and she and the other hunters quickly dispersed, blending into the shadows.

Dathon motioned for Soleia to follow behind him as they made the treacherous climb downward. A thick patch of passing cloud blotted out the moonlight illuminating the path but Dathon carefully picked out a trail as though he knew exactly where to go or perhaps his dragon eyes enhanced in the darkness.

The den ridge was even higher than the one at Cavell. Soleia couldn't help but gaze around in wonder. She had glimpsed it for a moment when she shared Dathon's eyes. It would have been so beautiful in the daytime with the striated layers of the surrounding mountains in different shades of red, the pink cliffs with the dark greenery sprinkled across the endless rocky landscape. She could understand why the dragons felt at home here. This was their sky.

Moving closer to the courtyard, Soleia felt a sudden tug on her hand when Dathon paused in mid-stride, catching sight of some markings having been gouged out of a rock face. His eyes narrowed as if in puzzlement or curiosity.

She gave him a prompting look. *What?*

But he just shook his head and beckoned her forward once more.

They were sneaking toward the same crevice the dragon from earlier had disappeared into. Soleia took care to brace her back against the wall to make sure they wouldn't be spotted if any more creatures arrived on the landing.

Slipping into the crevice led to a long corridor going deeper into the den. The corridor was narrow and tall, but with not much brisk wind flowing through, the same way in must be the same out—the only way out.

The dragons were obviously not expecting any intruders from so high up. There were no sentries inside but as they approached a bit of light up ahead, muffled voices—quite a few voices—echoed against the stone walls.

Soleia's stomach turned in dread. They were approaching the belly of the dragon's den. She glanced back at the darkened tunnel, her instincts screaming at her to run back the other way, but she braced herself. She had to complete the mission or she wouldn't get the antidote. She only hoped they weren't about to walk into a trap.

Dathon crept against the wall beside her as they inched closer to the flickering light coming out of a doorway, and when Soleia spied one of the dragons walking out of the room, she jerked back to brace against the wall again. But luckily, the individual deviated to head the opposite way and didn't see them.

Soleia tapped on Dathon's shoulder to indicate that they should pursue and strike him down.

Dathon peered back but then met her gaze with a shake of his head. Instead, he put a finger to his lips.

She furrowed her eyebrows in puzzlement. Although before she could even think to whisper her question, he motioned her forward, and the two of them braced by one side of the doorway.

Soleia peeked over his shoulder to see.

The den cavern was a lot like the entryway cavern at Cavell except it was a mere fraction of its size. It had a high ceiling, the room lit up by several lamps and torches mounted against the walls.

There was a stone hearth but it was not lit. Soleia was unsure if it had just been neglected or if in fact, these dragons did not require heat.

Given that the cavern had probably been set up some fifty years ago, there was possibly about that many years' worth of clutter and shiny trinkets adorning the rickety shelves in the wall crevices. Several stacks of books and an assortment of weapons were haphazardly piled up, dirty pots and jars, barrels overfilled with gold coins lay about.

Soleia spotted a makeshift dagger target practice board on the wall beside a panel for keeping score that was full of scratches.

Not to mention the half a dozen dragons in their human form lounging about the cavern. One of them had her feet propped up on the table as she examined some nicks in her dagger, her hand occasionally diving into a bowl of seeds. Two others were engrossed in a rudimentary board game while another one with fiery red hair was sitting by the window involved in a book.

The scene calling back to many quiet evenings at Ipera, Soleia thought the dragons looked no more a threat to anyone than...regular Fae.

Dathon's eyes were darting from one corner of the room to the other as if he was looking for something or someone, or possibly he was strategizing in his head how they should deal with the dragons.

"Follow my lead," he whispered in Soleia's ear. He let go of her hand, his fingers moving to encircle her wrist instead and he tugged her behind him. Adjusting his posture to his full height and with his chin up, Dathon so very casually and blatantly stepped across the threshold to stand in the middle of the cavern.

The redhead reading a book glanced up for a second, glimpsing the two of them before his eyes popped way open. His mouth dropped, and his book toppled on the floor with a thump before he immediately fell to one knee and bent his head.

Soleia blinked in surprise when as if a wave of alarm had reverberated throughout the room, the rest of the dragons alerted to the commotion, and one by one, each of them followed suit, bowing low to the ground.

But the young dragon's next words shocked Soleia even more.

"Your royal highness, where have you been?"

A shadow had fallen over Dathon's form entirely, his eyebrows furrowed, his gold-red eyes dark and menacing. He growled in displeasure. "Long story, Amon. How is everyone?"

"We are all good, sire," he replied.

Heart pounding, Soleia's jaw dropped. She could barely make her mouth work. "You—You're...?"

Dathon turned to her with a devious chuckle and yanked on her wrist to shove her toward the others. One corner of his mouth turning up, he looked to Amon. "Gag her."

18

Missed Things

Sweat beading on her forehead from the effort, Soleia struggled against the rough ropes around her ankles and binding her wrists behind her but it was no use. Her eyes darted around from her spot on the cold floor in the corner. Her heart pounded in her chest as she tried to make sense of what the hell just happened.

With a haughty, almost bored half-smile on his face, Dathon was still greeting the other dragons—his people, embracing them, clapping their backs, clasping their hands, receiving their adulations.

He was their goddamned prince.

I am a prince from a faraway land, he had said. Soleia growled to herself. *You don't even know who I am.* Her chest was heavy. How many other things had he mentioned were in fact true that she had just taken for a flat-out lie?

For a change, Soleia wished her hands were unbound just so she could slap her own self.

Several of Dathon's greeters didn't speak and Soleia figured they were communicating using only their thoughts again just as they had when the dragons had attacked them the first time in the desert. But why had they attacked if they were indeed his people? It made even less sense.

It might have been a side effect of Therin's poison but her head whirled with confusion. What in the hell was going on?

Dathon gestured his arm to one side. "There is one intruder targeting the tower sentries and three others likely on the desert floor." With his instructions clear and efficient, a couple of dragons jumped to do his bidding.

Amon was staring up at his face as though still in a marvel that he was among them. "Elias said they found you in the desert and that you were protecting this Fae."

Dathon snarled. "I was *not* protecting the Fae! I was merely biding my time. I knew I needed to gain their trust so I could escape."

Even though it was futile, Soleia struggled even harder against the ropes. She severely wanted to punch Dathon in the face. She wished she could cut him with more than her glare but aside from the fact that the dragons had taken her weapons, Dathon hadn't looked back at her once since he had revealed himself.

Amon wrinkled his nose as he studied Soleia's countenance. "This one's got a mean glare on her."

"I would if I was deceived too," Dathon huffed.

Trying to appear unintimidated, Soleia sneered through

her gag. Hell and damn, if she could but utter the binding word right then, she could hold Dathon's spirit hostage in exchange for her release. But of course, he already knew that.

"Should we just kill her?"

"Fool," Dathon snapped. "Why else would I have kept her alive until now? This evil Fae has put a curse on me. If she dies, I might never be free of it. I need to break this curse once and for all."

"How can we remove it?"

"We need to get the mage to remove the binding first."

"Perhaps the curse will break if she dies."

"Or perhaps it will never break if she dies. I am not willing to take that chance." He huffed, "Besides, she and her people have put me through hell for the last—I can't even remember how long. And if anyone's going to kill her, it's going to be me." His eyes flashed. "She's *mine*."

That was when Dathon finally slid a furtive glance her way. It was only for a split second before he immediately averted his gaze but she thought she caught a glimpse of a pointed meaningful flicker in his hardened expression.

What the—?

Soleia narrowed her eyes, watching Dathon mingle with his people as she tried to glean more clues to explain his behavior.

Follow my lead, he'd said right before they entered.

Could Dathon possibly be...?

Her eyebrows furrowed deep in thought.

Was he...merely putting up a front and lying to trick the dragons?

Soleia tried to take a deep breath. If that were the case and he was play-acting a role, he was doing it superbly. Or, of course, quite possibly, Soleia was also now beginning to seriously hallucinate from the poison. He was an evil dragon after all.

Or was he, really?

Goddammit.

Either way, she still needed to be extra vigilant.

The dragon who had been snacking sat back down at the table even as she sneered in Soleia's direction. "Arrogant Fae," she spat. "Bless the mother you were able to escape them after all this time, my lord."

"It wasn't that hard," Dathon drawled. "It just took a bit longer than I thought. These Fae are quite skilled with...distractions."

At that remark, despite the situation, Soleia couldn't help a roll of her eyes.

A scuffle at the end of the room saw Naz, Otto, and the other two hunters dragged in and shoved to the floor. Naz's eyes widened to see Soleia bound and gagged in the corner before she turned her enraged gaze up toward Dathon.

She could almost hear Naz's snide knowing retort about the treachery of dragons. And unfortunately, Soleia was unable to let her in on the potential deception. She also recognized the vile, vengeful look in Naz's eyes. The hunter was not going to be appeased either way.

Following the captives, the dragons had come through another crevice tunnel from the opposite side of the room along with one other.

"Good gods, as I live and breathe."

The voice made Dathon turn, his eyes already lit up with pleasure.

A beautiful young woman with porcelain skin and cropped, silvery white hair had walked in with a bemused smile on her face. She wore black armor with glimmering tiles, the same as the rest of the dragons, except for the leather belt holding an assortment of shiny metal daggers around her slender hips.

The relief in Dathon's tone was immeasurable even as he rushed in for an embrace. "Mina, you're alive."

Soleia's eyebrows snapped together. What the damn hell—?

Mina pulled back to grin at him. "I cannot believe I am seeing you again after such a long time, your highness. Are my eyes deceiving me?"

Dathon returned her grin, clasping her hands in his. "Mina," he began again as if in wonder or pride. "Are you in charge of this den now? I could barely believe it when I saw your mark by the courtyard."

"It has been a long few decades, sire," she relayed.

Soleia narrowed her eyes. The woman was too young to be his mother. Too old to be his daughter. Could she be Dathon's sister? Although apart from the hair, they looked nothing alike. Perhaps a cousin or simply a comrade? Mate? Soleia's nose itched in irritation at the compelling need to know.

"I thought I heard a report from someone having sighted you near the Outlands the other day. But I thought after fifty years, it was impossible." The woman glanced down, wrinkling her nose in loathing as she trailed her fingers down his one arm, noting the many new scars marked there. "They have been bleeding you."

At that, Soleia's chest ached with remorse. *She* had been bleeding him for possibly no other reason than her own vanity.

Dathon pulled away. "Never mind that."

Mina gave him an expectant look, her voice lowering slightly. "Where have you been? Gareth just left for home. He would have wanted to see you safe and alive."

Dathon's face sobered instantly. "Didn't Gareth tell you where I was?"

Mina shrugged. "We all thought you were dead. Gareth said you were lost to the Fae lands."

His expression faded. "I was... But I can explain that later." He shook his head briskly to change the subject before tilting his head in question. "Did you say Gareth just left for home? How? The spheres of protection..."

Mina's eyes widened in marveling. "Gareth has been experimenting with powerful magic enhancers for decades, amassing amulets and spells to be able to cross the spheres. It's how he can go back and forth through the Outlands barriers. However, his current magic doesn't yet allow him to enter any of the other realms. He wishes that we could collect more magical totems so that soon we may all be able to go home."

The fleeting melancholy look on her face struck Soleia as it bore close similarity to what she had glimpsed from Dathon's countenance back at Cavell.

Home. That was all they really wanted.

But something else from Mina's words had captured Dathon's attention and his eyes narrowed. "Tell me, have you some manner of legendary treasure here?"

Mina scrunched up her cute, little nose to recall. "Why,

yes, I think. It's a curious little artifact that Gareth stole from a seer." She glanced around the dark space. "It should be around here somewhere."

She moved around the den, carelessly lifting pot lids and turning over scraps of fabric and paper to peek underneath. "Gareth has not had time to study its capabilities fully as of yet but he believes the artifact may enhance his current magic. But more importantly," she added with an almost involuntary scowl, "he hopes it might restore our abilities since the dwindling magic of the land now denies us our fire."

Almost in aghast, Dathon's eyebrows rose at the revelation. "You have no fire."

Soleia's eyes widened in surprise too. That must have been why those first group of dragons in the desert didn't just burn them to a crisp the first time. It could also explain why any desert communities at all have survived this long. She could only imagine what destruction would befall Cavell and the entirety of the Outlands if the dragons had access to their most potent weapon.

Rueful, Mina shook her head. "No."

Regret slashing his face, Dathon frowned. "I am sorry it has been so hard on you all these years."

"It wasn't easy at the start," she confessed, "but Gareth has been taking care of us, making sure we are all fed and safe and have everything we need."

"By stealing from the desert communities?"

Mina pursed her lips noting the veiled affront in his tone. "Would you have us all starve instead? These ruthless desert Fae already hunt us down daily. They wish to kill us! We have no fire, barely any magic. We've only done our best to survive. You said so yourself, we are the sacred people. This land was laid out for us. We need only take what is already ours."

Soleia thought she caught Dathon hiding a flinch.

But Mina noticed as well. She studied him with a critical look. "What's wrong with you? Seriously, where have you disappeared to all these years? Did you get some kind of doctrine drilled into your thick head?"

Looking away, Dathon grunted again. "Again, a story I must tell another time." He ran his hands through his hair. "Listen, the hunters who captured me are after that treasure as well as the rest of the loot. Mina," he urged. "You need to leave, go somewhere far away. It's going to be too dangerous for you."

Soleia noted the deeply concerned, protective look on Dathon's face. Who the hell *was* this girl?

But Mina gave him a stubborn look. "You have definitely missed a lot, your royal highness. I am now as formidable a fighter as you."

He chuckled. "I can't wait to see it. But later."

She threw up her hands. "Besides, how might you think that they are any match for us? Especially now that you are back?"

Dathon cleared his throat, almost in self-admonition. "I am not quite myself yet. I've been...cursed." He lifted his hand with an indicatory touch at the string of beads around his neck.

Without bidding, Mina reached over to yank at them— hard.

Soleia almost surged up in her seat in objection.

But Dathon swatted Mina's hand away. "Ow! Stop it! It's not going to come off."

Mina's mouth curled in derision. "Oh, that's fun." She jerked her thumb back at Soleia in the corner. "Did *she* do that?"

And Soleia met her gaze with a red-hot, molten glare she hoped would expediently melt her pretty face.

Dathon rolled his eyes. "Yes."

Mina drew one of her daggers with a metallic swish. "Shall I end her for you?"

Soleia jumped in alarm, edging back further against the wall.

"Perhaps later." Dathon moved Mina's arm down before glancing around at the room again. "Right now, we need to make it appear as though the den is unguarded. Call in the sentries from outside. The dragon hunters are coming. But we'll surprise them with an attack of our own."

Mina whistled to get everyone's attention before turning back to Dathon, her eyes already gleaming. "This is going to be fun, isn't it?"

Dathon grinned in mock disbelief but then he shook his head. "Look, why don't you fly to the border and try to get a message through to Gareth? He needs to be alerted to what's happening as soon as possible."

She narrowed her eyes at him. "You're just trying to get rid of me again. You forget, I already know all your tricks."

He put his hand on her arm, his voice low. "Please, Mina. Do this for me."

Mina pursed her lips in displeasure, even with concession already in her eyes.

19

Loyalties

Moonlight poured in through the carved windows of the cavern.

Soleia felt faint.

Therin's poison was taking effect.

She cast a glance over at Naz and the others also bound and cowered in another corner. Soleia was certain that, like her, they would have been trying to get free of the ropes too but none of them had had any luck either.

Under the mistaken impression that their plan had succeeded, Therin and the first team of hunters had probably emerged from the nearby ridge and were already riding toward the den.

Her gaze darted from one corner of the den to the other. Mina's—rather Dathon's people were positioned and ready, set to ambush the hunters when they arrived.

Shit. This was how she was going to die.

Helpless. Alone.

The dragons seemed to have no plans for them except for being collateral damage in the battle against the hunters. Or perhaps Dathon had left instructions for their execution in the slim chance that they survived the skirmish.

As soon as the first fiery arrow was shot, the battle ensued with loud cries, shouts, and clamoring.

Soleia cringed, inching closer to the wall in an attempt to avoid the crossfire.

The second group of dragons lying in wait at strategic points across the cavern all shot up at once, and darkness exploded within the space as the dragons jumped out the windows, shifting forms, and taking to flight to attack the hunters from above.

When the black smoke cleared from Soleia's eyes, she almost gasped as she spotted Dathon. His eyebrows were furrowed intensely as he strode across the den. He was heading straight for her, a dagger in his hand.

Oh shit.

Pretend or not, his expression was fierce, dauntingly menacing.

His deception, if it was that, had seemed so real. Perhaps because it *was* real. This was who he really was. And she had known nothing about him. He had been hiding everything right from the start.

Perhaps he was finally going to make good on his word to kill her.

She tried to kick away and squeezed her eyes shut as he bent down with his dagger.

Her heart thundering in her chest and already anticipating

pain, her eyes flew open when instead the ropes binding her wrists came loose.

Dathon's face was close to hers. He lifted his hand to pull the gag down from her mouth.

Soleia jerked away, scrambling to reach for a weapon but Dathon grabbed her by the shoulders. She thrashed against him even as he pulled her up to stand, his arms braced around her.

"Soleia—for god's sake, stop! Stop fighting me!"

"Let me go! You arrogant, lying—"

He clamped his hand over her mouth so she couldn't speak the binding word. Her rants continued muffled in his hand. He had to raise his voice for her to hear. "It was a ruse, Soleia! I'm on your side. Now shut the hell up and stop fighting me! We've still got work to do."

She was heaving, her eyes ablaze before she turned down her rage. She blinked a few times to clear the anger from her mind.

She was right?

"I thought you would understand," he explained. "I had to pretend to do that. In case you didn't notice, my people hate Fae. They would have killed you on sight. They believed me dead. They would have thought I was either an apparition or been bewitched and killed me too. Now let's get out of here while everyone else is occupied fighting, shall we? Okay?" He raised his eyebrows in a prompt again before slowly lowering his hand from her mouth. "Alright...?"

She kept her glare on him, still evening out her breathing, but she quelled her protest, merely shrugging away to straighten up as Dathon bent to cut the ropes around her ankles.

He hurried to release Naz and the others, gesturing to several sacks by the window. "I've set aside some of the gold and trinkets you can take back to your people—," he was saying but as soon as Dathon had released Naz's bindings, the hunter leaped at him, knocking him to the floor, her hands grabbing for his throat.

"Naz!" Soleia cried out, already moving to intervene but Dathon put his hand up for her to stop. He wasn't going to resist.

He met Naz's gaze evenly, struggling to force the words out of his mouth as she tried to choke him. "Do you—want to waste more time fighting me—or wouldn't you rather—help your friends out there?"

Naz gritted her teeth and after a moment of hesitation, she let out an aggravated groan so loud it resonated down the narrow cavern corridors. But her grip around Dathon's neck slackened and she jumped to her feet. With a quick motion of her arm, she barked at the others. "Let's go. Therin needs us."

And with that, the hunters set to securing the rig to make their way down the ridge with the sacks of loot on their backs and they leaped out of view in flat seconds.

Clutching at his neck, Dathon straightened up. He turned to Soleia, almost flinching at the deep frown of animosity on her face.

Her chest still ached at his betrayal, feigned or otherwise. Her shredded pride refused to play the fool one more time. "How do I know you're not still lying to me right now?"

Dathon's eyes were a turbulent storm of helplessness. He visibly swallowed. "You don't," he rasped his plea. "Soleia..." He moved to approach her when there was a shout from outside.

Dathon barely had time to glance over his shoulder to note the fire-laden metal mold coast through the carved balcony, rattle, and roll on the floor. His eyes bulging wide, he leaped to cover Soleia just as there was an explosion.

Soleia recoiled in terror. Her head roared from the blast, she thought her eardrums would burst. With such an explosive force, she half expected to be riddled with metal shards, bleeding to death on the floor, quite possibly in several pieces.

But aside from the immense fleeting trembling in the stone floor beneath her, she felt no pain. And when she tentatively peered through her eyelashes, there was instead a faint, golden glimmer surrounding her.

Enormous wings had unfurled from Dathon's shoulders. They had wrapped around them, saving them from the blast. Even the noise from the fighting sounded muted from beyond the protective enclosure and it was as though there was no world beyond his fierce embrace.

Dathon pulled away just enough to meet her astonished gaze.

"How..." Still heaving, she could barely form words, a combination of shock and fatigue as she stared up at the golden cocoon. "What..."

He was just as surprised. "My... You...released my wings to protect us."

She blinked. She didn't know she could do that, let alone

that Dathon could transform partway. She was so stunned that she almost couldn't speak. "A-Are you hurt?"

He broke a smile as he reassured her. "No."

Soleia's eyes still wide, she marveled at the glow coming from his beautiful wings before she turned to study the gold light reflected in his eyes.

If not for his wings, Dathon would have died trying to protect her.

He had helped save her village when he had absolutely no reason to. He could have caught her off-guard and killed her at any time in the desert. He could have simply let the dragons take her away. He could have abandoned her the moment he'd overcome the spell of the curse beads but instead, he had stayed by her side and helped her harness her stubborn magic.

Whatever lies Dathon had told her, she couldn't deny one thing. He was on her side.

And despite her breathing getting more difficult, Soleia admitted, "It seems the curse beads know my truth. I trust your actions, if not your words."

Relief flooded Dathon's face at her words. Heaving with anticipation, he brushed a stray lock of her back from her face, his roughened fingers grazing her cheek and lingering there for a moment. His desire plain and his gaze pinned to her lips, his voice almost shook as he tried to rein in his control. "There's no time now. But when this is all over, I am going to make it up to you. I promise."

Still feeling faint, she gave him a wan smile. "I need to...not die first."

Dathon grinned as he helped her straighten up. "On it."

When Dathon's wings unwrapped from around them, the damage to the cavern was revealed. Smoke and debris sprinkled the air from the gaping hole having blown out one side of the den cavern. The large table had tumbled to one side. Everything in the room was in tatters, cracked barrels and pots spilled gold coins across the stone floor.

It could have also been the shock but Soleia's knees buckled the moment she tried to stand.

Dathon's forehead creased. "We need to get you that antidote." He scooped Soleia up in his arms and moved toward the hole in the wall to jump straight off.

Soleia's stomach rose and dropped as Dathon spread his wings. The wind whipping at her face at the speed of their descent, she tightened her grip around his neck even as his hold around her was firm and sure.

Studying the intensity in his eyes, the hard set of his jaw, Soleia's stomach fluttered again. His expansive wings flapped and stretched to safely glide them both the hundred or so yards straight down to the desert floor.

When Dathon landed on the ground with a hard thump, he gave a quick shrug and his wings folded back up into his powerful figure, out of sight once more. Soleia shivered at the thrill. She was going to have to remember to ask Dathon to show her that again later.

Dathon was solely focused on the mission. He cast a sweeping glance at the surroundings to spot Therin. "I don't see him."

The bottom of the ridge was littered with chunks of rock and debris, amidst which were a handful of dragons in human form having engaged Cavell's hunters. Metal clashing, the whooshing of arrows, and staunch shouts of fighting filled the din. Meanwhile, about a dozen hunters on horses were chasing or successfully leading away several flying dragon beasts toward the south.

Half a dozen bodies lay on the ground but Soleia couldn't detect if they were only injured or dead, hunters or dragons. Nauseous, she clutched at her stomach. She was partly responsible for having brought death and destruction to both these peoples. And perhaps now she was paying the price.

A shrieking dragon soared overhead and Soleia thought it was going to head straight for them but a fresh lot of arrows falling from the sky chased the dragon away.

When Soleia looked up, it was to see Callan riding toward them on Boots and her eyes lit up. Despite his deception, she still couldn't help the relief knowing he was safe and alive. She couldn't bear to hold a grudge against him. Soleia knew what he had done he had out of loyalty even if misplaced. He would always be her brother.

Boots neighed as though recognizing Soleia and screeched to a stop right before them.

"Soleia!" Callan cried out as he dismounted to approach her.

His face red, Dathon set Soleia down and he charged forward to cover her with another roar. "Leave her alone!"

Undaunted despite the exhaustion in his eyes, Callan tried to push past Dathon's forbidding form, craning his neck to meet Soleia's eye. "She's fading fast," he noted.

Dathon pushed him back, giving him a glare, his tone deep

and firm. "You did this to her. If you are not here to deliver the antidote, I suggest you leave right now. Otherwise, you have no idea the pleasure I will have shredding you to pieces."

Callan looked more than surprised at his sentiment. "Are you trying to save her?"

Dathon growled. "If she dies, *everybody* dies." His tone made it clear his directive was not a mere threat.

Callan's forehead creased but he met Dathon's steely gaze in understanding. He gestured his arm toward one side of the canyon. "Therin is this way."

With Soleia heaped on top of Boots once more, they set out for the western base of the den as Callan directed where Therin, Naz, and Otto were loading the sacks of gold onto a contingent of horses while many of the hunters had the dragons preoccupied.

Naz must have revealed Dathon's deception to Therin. Upon catching sight of their arrival, Therin's eyes darkened in molten rage. Stomping forward, he instantly drew his sword, rushing toward Dathon but Callan held him back.

Therin darted a glance up at Soleia, a weak heap on the horse. "I should have known better than to believe a pathetic mage could keep a monster in check. Are you happy now, little mage? Because of you, many of my people will die today."

Dathon snapped in fury, "You should have never involved her in any of this."

"I'm not talking to you, you evil beast," Therin spat out.

"Therin, we're good to go," Naz cut in.

Therin acknowledged her with a nod, giving a whistle and waving his arms in a signal to the others to move out.

Dathon's face was still dark. "I have provided you enough

of the gold to last your people through the cold season. I will personally see to it that the dragons do not harass the desert communities any longer. Now give me the antidote. There's no sense letting her die now."

Turning on his heel, Therin hissed. "Tough luck, dragon."

Dathon pounced forward but with a snap of Callan's hand, a sharp gust of wind sent Dathon staggering back again.

But even as Callan stepped in the way, he visibly swallowed hard and his eyebrows furrowed deep. There was a turbulent conflict in his eyes as a battle for his loyalties raged within him.

"Callan, move the hell aside," Dathon urged. "I know how much you mean to Soleia but if I have to go through you, we both know I will kill you."

Therin hopped up on his horse, his remark snide. "Come on, Callan. Don't let your pity run you weak."

Dathon's eyes flared. "You're going to kill her!"

Soleia slumped on the saddle. She tried to reach for Callan's hand. "Callan..."

Callan balled up his fists at his sides, his face contorting with tension.

Therin narrowed his eyes at Callan, mocking his hesitation as his horse walked a tight circle. "You owe me your life, boy, or have you forgotten? If you think betrayal is taken lightly among our people, you are severely mistaken. Now, enough of this nonsense and let's go before all those flying devils come back." Then he kicked his horse and rode off.

Callan shot another hesitant look over at Soleia. He squeezed his eyes shut for a moment before jumping onto a spare horse and spinning around to follow Therin.

"No!" Dathon growled in anger but before he could pursue them, Soleia grabbed his arm.

"Dathon—" *It's no use*, she wanted to say. Soleia was well aware of what a life debt meant and even as she wished Callan could free himself from his obligations to Therin, it was hopeless to intercede.

A loud cry dragged their attention back toward the leaving team of horses. For a moment, it wasn't clear what was going on until Callan's figure leaped off his horse to knock Therin off of his.

Callan was grabbing at Therin's cloak, looking for something.

The horses neighing loudly, the two struggled on the ground for a few moments before Callan raised his hand and a sharp blast of wind blew Therin away.

The old man stumbled back on the sand, furiously scrambling back to his feet, right before one of the winged beasts swooped low, and with a loud screech, grabbed Therin in its talons.

Eyes wide, Soleia nearly gasped in horror but they could only watch as the dragon whipped across the sky with its captive, disappearing into the clouds.

Callan returned with a noise of hooves, his arm already outstretched. He had retrieved the antidote from Therin. Wasting no time at all, Dathon grabbed the vial of yellow liquid from Callan's hand and tipped the antidote into Soleia's mouth. His eyes furtively watched her face for signs of improvement.

Callan walked his horse in a circle. "You need to get out of here," he advised in between breaths. "Can she portal?"

"She can barely walk." Dathon's face was still wrinkled with worry. Despite having successfully administered the antidote, his hands still shook as if in a panic that it was too late.

"Ride, don't fly. It will be easier to hide." Callan's face still wrought with remorse, he raised his hand with a wave, the motion rippling the air as of a magical shroud. "I'll make sure you are not tracked. Leave this place. Find your way back to Ipera. I hope you make it."

The warmth of the antidote was already spreading through her insides. Soleia's chest swelled with gratitude and relief, she met Callan's gaze without words.

But Callan understood. He reached his hand up to her cheek and despite himself, he darted the most commanding glare Soleia had ever seen him wear toward Dathon as he ordered, "Take care of her."

Dathon merely grunted, reaching for Boots' reins.

"Callan," Soleia managed to call out.

He glanced up to meet her meaningful gaze one last time.

"I had better...see you again," she bid with as much authority in her tone as she could muster.

A ghost of a smile appeared on Callan's lips before he kicked off "*Hya!*" and was soon out of sight with the dust cloud trailing behind him.

Dathon turned to hop up onto the saddle. "Shift over."

"Why didn't...two horses?" Soleia protested weakly.

Dathon rolled his eyes. "Just shut up and move."

20

Old Debts

The fever Soleia was running had broken by the time they stopped to rest.

Just beyond the tree line where they set down lay the western ranges and the treacherous mountain pass leading to the next realm.

Dathon didn't want to make a fire in case it attracted predators or gave away their location since Callan's magical shroud had worn off.

Propped against a rock pedestal on the blanket in the clearing, Soleia watched Dathon rub Boots down beside an overgrown tree. Her trust in him was still fairly new. It was easy to slip into overthinking or second-guessing. And after their ordeal, she had so many questions but she wanted to conserve her energy. There was still quite a long way to go.

Also, her throat was sandpaper.

Of course, she couldn't help herself.

"So that was intense," she rasped.

Dathon didn't turn around.

"And you *were* their leader."

It wasn't really a question.

She dropped her gaze. His deception back at the den still sent tremors of foreboding within her. Perhaps because it was a little too close to the truth. "Back there...you wouldn't even look at me."

When Dathon spun, his face was crumpled. "I am sorry. I had to be true to the part I was playing. I couldn't risk them reading my mind." He paused, a shadow of remorse flitting past his face. "And—I couldn't bear to look at you like that. To be the cause of your suffering. To be reminded of what I used to be—what I still am. The monster from your legends."

Soleia's heart ached. "You thought this land was yours to take, to torment. You said that wasn't you. It *was* you."

Frustrated, he shook his head in protest as he began to pace. "No, it's not me. I mean I've..." he trailed off. He ran his hands through his hair in resignation. "I mean, alright, let's say I *was* an arrogant and privileged ass."

"I'm so glad you agree."

"It's not something I'm proud of," he admitted. "But I'm not now. At least not anymore. I meant what I said to Therin. I will ensure that none of the desert communities are harassed by the den dragons any longer." His eyebrows furrowed when he met her gaze. "Do you believe me?"

Soleia was no match for the desperate sincerity in his eyes. She let out a sigh, willing all her tension to melt away. She simply nodded.

Dathon gave her an appreciative half-smile but then

averted his gaze again. "Though I'm afraid I can't guarantee this about all the dragons. I am pretty sure Gareth's dragons —those ones that attacked us in the desert the first time, have likely gone rogue. They must guard the barrier on the Outlands side, waiting for his return."

"Who is Gareth?" Soleia recalled the name having been mentioned by Mina.

"Gareth is..." His eyes darkened. "He *was* my best friend. My cousin. Almost my brother." He shook his head. "Though I had been aware for quite some time that he had grander designs for himself, I quite naively thought his loyalties ran deeper than to plot against me. I suppose he finally lucked into the opportunity to usurp my position."

He groaned under his breath. "He's definitely not looking for a happy family reunion. I am certain Gareth has made it clear he wanted me to remain dead or disappeared."

Soleia furrowed her eyebrows. "You were looking for him at the den," she realized. "Before you revealed yourself. You wanted to check if the rogue dragons were there."

He nodded. "I didn't know who was running the den after fifty years. I didn't know Mina was alive. I had to make sure she was safe. Otherwise, I would have led the den breach myself."

Soleia bit her lip. She had put off asking for the entire ride. "Who is Mina?"

Dathon started to respond, "Mina is my—" but then he stopped and shot her a look, a hint of amusement tugging at the corner of his mouth.

She watched him warily. "What?"

His mood shifting, it looked like he was suppressing a

smirk. "Mina...is my cousin. Gareth's sister," he supplied. "We don't have the sort of relationship that perhaps you are thinking about. She is also like a sister to me."

Despite the weight on her chest easing at the revelation of Mina's identity, Soleia shifted in her seat. "What? I didn't say anything."

His stare was making her uncomfortable. Clearing her throat, Soleia made an effort to get up. She walked up to tend to Boots so as not to have to meet Dathon's eyes. "That was a long ride for Boots," she began. "He will need quite a bit more water than what we have."

"Why are you changing the subject?"

From this mere tone, Soleia could almost feel the cocky grin that was back on his face without having to see it. *So annoying.* She rolled her eyes but didn't oblige him with a response.

"I do so enjoy jealousy," Dathon drawled. "Did you know Mina is very skilled with daggers? I've always enjoyed her company." Then his voice came from closer behind her. "Would it bother you if I said I find her quite beautiful?"

Soleia held back several barbed comments that popped to mind as that was exactly the rise he wanted out of her. But Dathon had forgotten one vital thing. Something she knew would knock the wind right out of his wings.

When she finally replied, Soleia made her teasing chuckle wry. "Far from it," she noted, giving him a pointed glance over her shoulder. "If you do so recall, I am promised to be mated to one of our village warriors."

His face darkening instantly, Dathon winced at the recollection.

With a haughty tone, she went on, "I expect the arrangements will be made as soon as I return to Ipera. Juric is a great warrior. I hear he's also terribly clever with knives. And he's always favored me. I know I didn't seem keen on the match at first but Juric will be vastly elated once I consent to be—" She whirled around to step away but he caught her arm.

"You belong to me." His declaration came out as half a growl.

Despite her heart pounding, she gave him a flat look. "Is that right? How do you figure?"

"You owe me your life," he pointed out.

She stuck her chin up. "And you owe me yours."

His eyes narrowed at her rationale.

Dathon had indeed saved her life again but she had also saved his times over. Soleia couldn't reckon if it meant that they were in fact even or if it instead indicated a doubling down on their earlier debts.

A sharp tug brought her closer to him and she countered his searing glare with a steely one of her own. Soleia was trying not to start heaving but she didn't attempt to struggle. "Unhand me."

His eyes flashed, measuring the challenging look on her face, but he wasn't deterred. He lifted his other hand to touch her cheek. His gaze dropping to her mouth, he let his fingers travel there to stroke her lips, and when he looked up to meet her ice blue gaze again, there was no mistaking the heated need in his eyes.

The same need pulsing through her veins, her breathing become ragged. "What exactly do you think you're doing?" she prompted, loading as much mocking in her tone as she could despite the fluttery anticipation deep in her core.

He swallowed hard, his eyes already glazed. His heavy-lidded gaze pinned on her mouth once more and his voice lowered at his next statement. "I am offering you my heart."

Her eyes widened the slightest bit at his candor.

"—if you still want it."

The deep, sultry sound of his voice wrapped warmly around her and gave her chills at the same time.

Her body crushed against his, his scent making her light-headed, his breath hot on her face.

Dathon pressed his thumb down against her full lower lip, teasing her mouth open, and the low growl that escaped him turned her insides liquid.

Her chest heaved against his. She couldn't stop staring at his mouth, couldn't stop imagining how his soft lips might feel on hers, his hands rough in her hair...

"I want it."

His control shattered with a rumbling groan. He bent his head and took her open mouth in his.

She still gasped at his urgency. Her parted lips let his tongue easily slide inside her mouth, seeking hers, stroking, tangling, sharing his heat with her, into her.

He gripped her chin in one hand so she could receive his searing kiss, tilting her head back to give him better access.

Her eyes squeezing shut, she moaned in his mouth. Every nerve in her body sang, her whole body flushed hot, and something pent up deep inside her released at the same time that a deeper need grew.

This. Yes. This.

Dathon couldn't get enough. He devoured her, claimed her, his hands shifting around her head, her back, her neck. He gave a sharp, firm tug on her braid which only set her on fire even more.

Soleia dug her fingers in his hair, and when she tugged back, he growled in her mouth, his kisses growing wilder, rougher.

Encouraged by his response, she devoured him back just as fiercely. She clutched at the front of his tunic, pressing against his hard chest. She could barely breathe but she didn't care. She wanted to drown in him, in his hunger, in his strength.

Then Soleia's knees weakened—in fatigue.

Noticing her eyelids flutter, Dathon stilled against her. And with a groan of considerable effort, he pulled back, breathless, his posture relaxing. "Alright, Princess..." he soothed. "Time for bed."

Her face still flushed, Soleia managed a half-smile. "Are you going to make me see stars now?"

Dathon chuckled. "Not that kind of bed. You're still weak from the poison. You need to recover." Still evening out his heavy breathing, he met her gaze. "But afterward, I guarantee you, I will definitely make you see stars."

Soleia scoffed in mocking as she let him lay her back down on the blanket.

He was going to step away when she caught his arm.

"Keep me warm."

Dathon chuckled again deep in his throat but obliged her invitation and she rolled to one side so he could lie beside her on the blanket.

He shifted until he was arched against the line of her back. His hand moved down to prop upon her hip as he fit himself closer, cradling the curve of her body with his, his delicious warmth enveloping her.

Soleia took a deep, satisfied breath. She trailed her fingertips down the muscled forearm tucked under hers and her eyebrows furrowed at her afterthought. "Hey, does this mean you're actually a prince?" she prompted. "As in, at some point, you're going to inherit a throne?"

His chest rose and the rumble in his chest as he responded vibrated within her as well. "Yes. Princess…"

His lips brushing her ear at the whispered words sent chills throughout her body but Soleia's heart nearly stopped. Even as she had asked the question offhand, his simple response carried so much weight, so much meaning, her throat instantly went dry.

Princess…

Her skin suddenly prickled in an undefined uneasiness.

"You know, since we left Cavell, I've been thinking—" Dathon started, the words still spoken by her ear, his fingers stroking up and down the bare skin on her arm ever so lightly.

Soleia perked up in alert. "Thinking? Thinking of what?"

"Well, I didn't believe for the longest time that it was possible but—"

"What? But what?" She shot out in sharp, short bursts.

He chuckled low, his shoulders shaking against her in mirth. "Well, if you would let me finish, I'll tell you."

Soleia's chest heaved in anticipation or…dread but she couldn't see his face so it was difficult to read his tone.

"I think you are the key."

And she stopped short.

Her eyebrows snapped together in confusion all over again. "What?"

"I knew it since you formed that portal up on the ridge," Dathon relayed with a tone of authority. "Having seen what you are capable of, I think you are the answer. Perhaps *you* can take down the spheres of protection on the Outlands and help my people get home."

All the blood drained from her face. "What?"

"Not only that. I think once you've harnessed your portal summoning abilities, you should be able to restore the magic and heal the land. Save Arcadia," Dathon declared. "Perhaps you could undo what Helene did altogether and put every-thing to right."

She sat upright to turn to him in disbelief. "Whoa, whoa, whoa."

He sat up to meet her gaze evenly. "I once thought I could do anything. It was a devastating blow to resign to the inevitable demise of the land my people were meant to protect. But perhaps we don't simply have to wait and watch the magic die. Perhaps you can help me can stop it. You can fix it." He reached out to cradle her cheek in his hand.

Her flinch away was nearly involuntary. "I can't do that." She pushed to straighten up in aghast, stepping back a few paces as if it distanced herself from the topic itself. "I'm not— I'm nowhere near that powerful. Besides, save Arcadia—that's —that's a big responsibility."

Dathon cast her a curious glance. "It is your responsibility."

She threw up her hands. "Why? Because it was my Great-aunt who ruined everything?" She groaned in complaint.

"What about my sister? She's the perfect one. What about literally *anyone* else? All of this stuff was just sprung on me. I wasn't supposed to do any of this."

His forehead creased in confusion. "Fine." He shrugged. "What did you think you were going to do after all this instead?"

"I was..."

Dathon studied her face. "You were going to run away again?" he guessed, unable to hide the ridicule in his tone.

Soleia grimaced. "Whatever I had planned, they were *my* plans," she snapped. "And I've been lucky enough to survive so far even with all this craziness. I sure as heck don't want to tempt fate trying to attempt any more miracles with this ridiculous magic."

Needing more space, she stepped back again, moving past Boots, past the nearby trees, her feet blindly carving out a path through the forest. She dropped her gaze, her chest constricting tight.

"Where are you going?" Dathon called after her in exasperation.

"I—I can't deal with this right now. I have to think."

"You mean run away?"

Her wide-eyed gaze met his knowing declaration but she bit her tongue.

Dathon pursed his lips. "Fine! When the going gets tough, you lie and run away. Isn't that what you do anyway?"

Seething as his words hit squarely home, Soleia spun around and didn't break stride. She walked faster, setting off into a run.

There was nowhere to go. Not to mention she really

couldn't leave Boots. But she just wanted to feel the brisk wind on her face since perhaps it would wake her up from this never-ending nightmare.

Of all the casting magic in the land, why did she have to be burdened with this one?

She reckoned she would have made a great fire mage. She would have apprenticed at one of the blacksmiths in the village. She would have loved to make weapons. If her family hadn't thought she had portal summoning abilities, would she have gone on to lead a normal life? She would have trained as a normal mage and never had to hide.

A wave of nausea hit her. It was too late now. It seemed no matter where she went, the fates kept throwing her the same hands regardless. What if there really was no escaping it?

Surrender.

Her mind battled with confusing thoughts. She had only ever wanted her freedom. Was she really good for nothing else except running away? How much of a coward was she?

She squeezed her eyes shut in annoyance at herself, but the next moment, she almost tripped on the rocky path as the sky was engulfed in pitch black.

Soleia's head whipped up to see several large dark shadows flying past above the trees and her stomach dropped to her toes.

They've found us.

She threw herself to the ground by a clump of bush hoping the ground was camouflage enough but the dragons hadn't spotted her. They were headed straight for the clearing a few yards away.

For Dathon.

Soleia could just make him out across the way having straightened up from their blanket on the ground. His shoulders were held back, his posture tight, alert.

He knew.

With a burst of black clouds, four dragons in human form emerged from the darkness just before one enormous dragon landed with a whump in the clearing in full form, snapping through branches, and swatting trees down.

Its obsidian scales glistened in the dim light, horns twisty and sharp, eyes black as death itself. But Soleia didn't have to wait for him to change to guess who he was.

Once he was done with his posturing, the black dragon burst into another inky haze and the figure of a tall man appeared. He had sleek ebony hair and jet-black eyes like his dragon and he merely met Dathon's gaze with a half-smile on his mouth.

After a moment, Dathon snorted. "And I never thought we'd be meeting this way, brother."

Gareth's tone was already bemused as he approached him. "Speaking out loud," he remarked with a nod. "He grows more and more Fae indeed."

Soleia figured Gareth must have been attempting to communicate with Dathon by mere thought but for whatever reason, Dathon had chosen for their conversation to be plain.

"I just didn't know if it was true. I had to see for myself. You are indeed alive, brother." Gareth cast a glance around. "But where is your Fae mistress?"

His question sailed through the trees, crisp and clear and Soleia's heart pounded in her chest and she crouched lower behind the bush.

Dathon gave two dragons a wary look as they approached to flank him before giving Gareth a steely look. "Gone."

Soleia held her breath. She realized Dathon could possibly be insisting on conversing out loud in case she was still nearby. She couldn't let them see her but she had to help Dathon somehow.

"Mina said the den was attacked. She said something smelled fishy but I just never thought…" Gareth's gaze seemed far away. "Then I come back to see the den all wrecked, the loot half gone. How could you do that to us? Betray your own people? Take sides with those—Fae." He made a face as if the mere word left a sour taste in his mouth.

Dathon tried to sidestep away but Gareth's henchmen grabbed him by the arms.

A fleeting shadow of bitterness crossed Gareth's dour face as he stepped closer. "You know, I never did mind all those years of being compared to you." He shook his head. "No, I looked up to you, Dathon. You were my hero. I wanted to *be* you. I did everything you said. I followed in your footsteps."

"And now I see you sympathizing with these inferior beings, mingling with Fae and humans." He cracked his neck as though the fact physically pained him. "It's disgusting!" He spat. "Don't you remember we are above them? We own this land!"

Dathon's lips pressed tight. "No, we don't. We have been tasked to protect it. There's a difference."

Gareth spun around, dismissing him with a wave. "Look, whatever. If you don't want to take your throne back, I'll gladly have it. I have been enjoying it for the past fifty years. What can I say? I'm comfortable."

"And this is what you do with all this power?" Dathon mocked. "Seriously, Gareth, you've had the throne for fifty years. What have you got to show for it? An isolated den that's barely surviving at the ends of the world, terrorized villages across the Outlands, worthless trinkets? Seems to me you are giving in too much to your animal nature's love of hoarding."

Gareth chuckled again. "Oh, your royal highness, you always did think in small terms." He sneered. "I have been seeking a treasure to make all my dreams come true. One that will make me even more powerful than you." The grin that returned to his face was smug. "And I think I've finally found it."

From underneath his tunic, he fished out a golden medallion hanging from a chain around his neck and it glinted in the faint light. "You have no idea how long I've been searching for one of these. I knew one was in the human realm, having been passed down for generations. I even thought it was at one of those little villages near the Mountain Lake you told me about but I checked there and found nothing."

His casual addendum made Dathon's eyes narrow. "What do you mean you checked there?" he wanted to know, the urgency in his tone growing. "You checked where, Gareth?"

"Those sacred villages with the secret entrance your little Fae girlfriend used to sneak you to. I followed her one day and she led me right to them. Total waste of time though. I only found a few trinkets—nothing of consequence." Then he chuckled. "Those people thought their flimsy gods would protect them. Well...I took care of that delusion."

Upon hearing that, Soleia's stomach turned over. *Oh dear*

god. She clapped her hand over her mouth as both nausea and rage simmered within her. It dawned on her what had happened fifty years ago. What had driven Helene to rage. What Oermilla had witnessed.

I've seen first-hand the destruction he is capable of. It won't stop until we are all destroyed...

"They were peaceful people—" Dathon's eyes bulged and he strained his captor's grasp on his arms as he pressed forward. "You... you destroyed... It was *you*," he declared. "Helene knew I was intrigued by those places. I told you about them in confidence. Nobody else knew! That's why she thought..." He looked like he'd been punched in the gut.

Then Dathon swallowed hard, his eyes lighting up again as the notion struck him. "And you told me to go..." he trailed off, averting his gaze. "You *knew* Helene would find out. You were counting on her reaction, her rage. You sent me back to the Fae lands knowing full well—"

Gareth rolled his eyes. "All the Fae are predictable. And what happened to you merely served as concrete proof to our people of how ruthless and unconscionable the Fae are. Honestly, I never considered this 'spheres of protection' scheme and getting our people trapped in the Outlands happening. I thought your Fae consort would've just killed you and saved me the trouble." A smirk laced his next prompt, "Have you been living there as their slave since?"

Growling low in fury, Dathon's lips curled. "I was bound to a tree, asleep for years."

Gareth burst out laughing, slapping his knee. "Oh, that's perfect. His royal highness was pinned to a tree, fully impotent, while time simply passed. Then it is indeed a miracle that our fearless leader is back among us. Something that will need rectifying soonest." He gestured to the goons holding onto Dathon and they tugged him back.

Dathon tried to struggle away. "You are a monster and a coward. You could never be a leader. You will always just be a sneaky traitor, copying all my moves, always being second-best."

That set Gareth off and he pounced on Dathon, grabbing him by the front of his shirt. "You arrogant ass," he growled. "Perhaps it is lucky after all. All these years and I still get a chance to kill you myself. Why don't you shift so we can settle this?"

Soleia's heart dropped to her toes. She had left Dathon cursed, unguarded, nearly defenseless.

Dathon tried to shrug him off. "I can't shift. The Fae have cursed me." He gestured to the beads around his neck. "If you want to kill me, just kill me."

"Cursed you? How?"

"That Fae woman I was with. I'm bound to her. She holds my dragon spirit. The only way to remove it is to get the elder Fae to undo the curse."

"Hmm, interesting..." Gareth stepped back. "Well, I'm not completely dishonorable to strike you down when you are a defenseless man. Besides, it won't be any fun if I don't see you squirming in your dragon form."

Soleia heaved in dread. There was no way she could take on six rogue dragons all by herself. She had no weapons. And even with Dathon's assistance they were still severely out-numbered. Sure, she had felt more confident with the hunters before but these were full-grown dragons of legend.

Think.

However, before Soleia could form any more schemes, rough hands grabbed her shoulders from behind to pull her up off the ground and she was faced with another dragon's surly glare.

Mina peered at her face, sniffing. "I thought I smelled something foul here." She flipped her short hair before whirling around. "I'm glad I didn't miss out on the opportunity of killing some Fae today."

Mina's murderous energy was quite similar to how Dathon had initially come across to Soleia that if the situation wasn't so dire, she would have laughed. But the two other dragons who had grabbed her by her arms dragged her toward the clearing and her scowl returned.

"Look what I found, Gareth," Mina announced as she approached the others.

"Soleia!" Dathon's eyes widened upon spotting them and he tried to pull away but Gareth's people held him back. "Mina." He met her steely gaze. "Mina, listen to me. You don't understand what's going on. You're making a big mistake."

Mina's face clouded over with sadness. Ironically, she must have felt the same betrayal that Soleia had felt when Callan turned. "You have been bewitched, brother," she spoke low, subdued. "You're the one who is suddenly sympathetic to the Fae. You're the one who has changed."

Gareth clapped his hands as Soleia was shoved forward. "Well, this is a lovely turn of events. Is this the Fae that holds your spirit?" He studied Soleia's form up and down with a glint in his eyes.

Dathon grunted but didn't reply.

Mina faced Gareth. "I heard from the others this one is a portal summoner."

"She's a what?" Gareth's eyes gleamed.

Soleia's heart thudded in her chest.

"A portal summoner."

Gareth's grin widened. "Like Helene." The eagerness in his eyes hinted at something brewing in his maniacal brain.

Something Soleia could tell was not going to bode well for her. She couldn't help but roll her eyes. *Here we go again.* "For god's sake, I'm *not* a portal summoner," she moaned. "I could barely do it the one time. It's not going to work anymore. Don't make me do it again."

"Well, we'll see about that." Gareth's grin had a mischievous tinge to it as he regarded Dathon with an airy sneer. "Since I just had a perfect idea. Why bother killing you when instead, I could own you?"

"What the hell are you talking about?" Dathon scoffed.

Gareth drawled, "I mean how boring would it be if I could just end your suffering right now? But what a lovely thing for me to have his royal highness himself as my pet."

Soleia's face paled. He couldn't mean...

Gareth turned to her again but his words were still directed to Dathon. "So if the only way to remove the curse is to get the Fae to undo it, I'm guessing we can also get the Fae to transfer the ownership of your curse to me."

Dathon's face darkened. "I'd rather die than be bound to you."

"I think you'll find nobody asked your opinion." He waved his arm as a gesture to the others to move out. "It seems we are going to the Fae lands."

"How?" Dathon grunted, struggling to get away from his captors once more to no avail. "Ipera is past the western ranges. There's no way to get there through the spheres of protection. Mina said you still can't cross to the other realms."

Gareth's eyes lit up. "Oh, you forgot about my new precious treasure." He grinned. "I think it's time for a little demonstration. I've been wanting to test this reliquary." He stepped closer to Soleia again. "And what a perfect specimen to try it out on."

Thrashing against his captors, Dathon's eyes widened. "What are you doing? Don't touch her."

"Dathon, really." Gareth looked astonished. "You really are protective of this one, aren't you? That's too bad."

Soleia's eyes bulged as she watched Gareth approach her but the other dragons' grasp was firm and her struggle to get away was futile.

Gareth reached one hand toward her, cold fingers clasping at her throat but he didn't squeeze. However, despite that, Soleia felt woozy and there was a burning sensation around her neck.

She clenched her teeth, groaning at the intensifying pain. She almost couldn't breathe.

What the hell was Gareth doing to her?

Mina and the other dragons merely watched, smug, wordless, marveling.

After a few more moments, her eyelids fluttering closed in the strain, Soleia's knees buckled. When she went slack against the dragons holding her, they let her slump to the ground.

Gareth straightened up with a howl. "Ahh, that feels fantastic!"

"Soleia, what's wrong?" Dathon struggled against his captors again. "Soleia, what's happening?"

"Unlike most of the talismans I've collected," Gareth began, "my new toy is a very unique type of magic enhancer. Guess what it lets me do." He raised his glowing hand level to his face and grinned in satisfaction as bluish-white sparks hovered above his palm—right before a small, swirling whorl made of a not-quite-liquid silvery sphere burst to life, flickering dazzling light across everyone's faces.

Soleia's eyes nearly popped out of her head.

Portal!

Gareth's eyes were just as wide in astonishment and malice. He closed his fist and the portal whooshed away, leaving the clearing just as dark as it was before. He let out a triumphant laugh then he licked his lips. "I'll tell you, she is one powerful mage, brother. Feels really..." He waved his hand in the air to add, "buzzy."

Soleia had a really good comeback for that but she couldn't even lift her cheek from the ground as she lay with her eyes half-closed. It appeared Gareth had decided not to drain her completely. She was still alive except she could only manage shallow breaths for the moment.

Dathon's near-crazed indignation reached a peak at seeing Soleia heaped on the ground and he struggled even harder against his captors that another dragon had to come forward to help hold him still. "Gareth, you coward, you leave her alone! You already have me."

"Relax! I only had a little taste," he assured. "Maybe I'll take the rest later. I guess there is a use for these Fae, after all."

If Soleia had enough strength left to throw up, she would have.

"Were you aware that the spheres of protection were made of the same type of energy magic as portals? I studied them quite a lot." Gareth stopped short to amend, "Or perhaps you already knew that being that it was your arrogant kinsman who erected these barriers. *Or* perhaps you are even more ignorant as I thought."

Heaving, Dathon's molten glare was pinned on Gareth, but his thoughts must have been too plain that Gareth raised his finger in warning. "Be careful, my brother. Now that I know what this Fae means to you, you should know better than to try anything untoward."

Gareth snapped his fingers and his people picked Soleia up from her heap on the ground. "How does it feel?" He peered at her face. "I'm going to slowly drain your magic, the same way your people drain our blood."

Even as Soleia wanted to sock him in the face, she couldn't respond. She barely had enough energy to glare at him.

"With this magic under my control, I should be able to break through the realm spheres on the western mountain range. And I can finally lead our people to escape this godforsaken realm." Gareth turned to Dathon and Mina. "Besides, what do you think I've been gathering all this magic for all these years? Our kind has been stuck in the Outlands for too long. Soon I'll have enough power to breach all the other realms and reclaim them as our people were meant to."

Dathon growled. "I'm going to kill you."

There was a catch on Gareth's smile as he considered his threat. "Maybe when you are my pet, I'll make you kill her." He grinned again. "Now then, I guess we have to go and pay a visit to an old Fae, don't we?"

And with that, he burst into a thick black haze, shifting back into his dragon form to lead the way through the western mountain pass.

To Ipera.

21

Family Reunion

Soleia couldn't see Gareth, couldn't see Dathon.

In the faint light of early morning, the low clouds prevented a clear view of the entire formation of monstrous dragons—nine so far that she could count, with Mina holding up the rear of his invading troop.

Mina's dragon was a slightly smaller, white creature with glittery scales. Soleia would have thought it quite pretty if she wasn't struggling in a net carried like a sack of potatoes in its talons as they sped through the air.

Soleia was still weak from Gareth's extraction of her magic. She could barely muster enough strength to gripe about her situation.

She had been captured by the evil dragons. She had lost all her weapons. Her favorite horse was left abandoned in the desert mountains. And now she was effectively accompanying a raiding party to most likely destroy her village, not to mention the entire realm.

A brilliant flash of light up ahead grabbed her attention and her gaze shot over to see a bright blue near-invisible boundary sphere momentarily flicker in mid-air amidst the western mountain pass beneath them.

It must have been the sphere of protection between this realm and the next. Soleia swallowed in dread. And the flicker must have been where Gareth had used *her magic* to break through into the Fae lands.

She watched the oscillating boundary warily as Mina and the rest of the dragons before her sped forward. The invisible wall was supposed to keep them out.

Soleia squeezed her eyes shut as they neared the threshold.

Such a protective barricade would have simply repelled anything trying to get in, even massive creatures such as dragons, but because of Gareth, Mina and all the dragons sailed through without issue.

Breathless in amazement, Soleia glanced back at the now-seeming harmless barrier. Her eyes were wide in awe of its sheer size. It stretched right from the bottom of the green valley upward past the mountain peaks before fading off indeterminately into the sky.

Great-aunt Helene had conjured that—and no doubt the multiple similar ones cutting divisions clear across the Arcadian continent.

Only one with such a mastery of that power... Access to that level of magic, reaching all across the land, was unheard of...

Chills ran up Soleia's spine.

Such power. Such incredible power.

It didn't take much longer for her to recognize the changing landscape. They were soaring over the foothills skirting the Fae lands and she could but spot the thick cursed forest toward the northern horizon.

But Gareth and the other dragons having had a considerable lead from Mina's dragon had afforded them the opportunity to inflict damage already glaringly and terribly evident.

Ipera's forest valley was under siege.

Screams rang in the chaos. People were running amok. Even the giant wraiths in the cursed forest were contending with the rogue dragons—and losing. The village landscape was nearly unrecognizable. Entire clusters of houses and assembly structures were either collapsed altogether or showed visible signs of significant damage, field crops were devastated, and traces of black smoke wafted up from different pockets throughout the valley.

Grasping the net surrounding her, Soleia gasped as Mina's dragon circled above the village square looking to land. But as she peered below, Soleia could already sight Gareth's black smoke as he shifted into his human form.

Soleia's panning gaze screeched to a stop upon spotting Dathon. His hands and feet were bound as he slumped in a heap beside Gareth's forbidding form while several Fae elders having already been captured by Gareth's rogues were laid out before him on the road in front of the temple.

Soleia's eyes widened as she recognized the frail figure of the Fae elder dragged forward.

Oma!

True to his word, Gareth's first order of business was extorting the means of transferring Dathon's curse ownership over to him.

But Soleia knew there was no way Oermilla would ever do such a thing. Her heart pounded in her chest. Oermilla was going to get herself killed.

Panicked, Soleia's eyes darted around furtively to look for Caelina or any of the village warriors in vain. She tugged desperately on the net holding her. "Mina! Get us down! Mina, please! Hurry, I have to help her!"

But her protest was futile. There was no way she could get out of her net. And Mina couldn't care less about the Fae.

Soaring closer to the ground, Soleia could see Gareth stomping unhappily. Oermilla was not cooperating as Soleia had fully expected.

Gareth let out a loud growl and approached her instead. He put his hand against the old woman's throat, much as he had done to Soleia.

Soleia's eyes widened as she cried out, "Oma! Please!"

By the time Mina landed and dropped Soleia still tangled up in her net, Oermilla's frail form had slumped to the ground.

"Take the others." Gareth waved carelessly as his attention was fixed on his affected hand once more. "I'll use them later."

Within seconds, the rogue dragons had dragged their captives away, some disappearing into a burst of clouds to take to the skies once again, and save the faint shouts of distant fighting, the village square fell quiet.

Except for Gareth, face glowing in satisfaction, he laughed.

"Well, that was a pretty good hit." He was trying to brag to Dathon but Dathon's gaze was pinned on Soleia who had fallen to her knees in anguish for her grandmother.

Tears streamed down her face. Still trapped in her net, Soleia was across the square from Oermilla but that didn't stop her from reaching her hand out in a desperate cry.

Oermilla was immobile, lying on her back on the stone path, her gaze raised to the sky. It seemed she was still conscious but it wasn't clear whether she would be for much longer.

Seeming unable to stand Soleia's grief-stricken weeping, Dathon shifted to his side on the ground. "Mina! Let Soleia go to her kin," he barked his order. "I will not believe that you have lost your compassion all these years."

Mina's eyes narrowed at him. She averted her gaze, not responding.

But Gareth was only focused on one thing. His eyes gleaming, he cast Mina a brief look. "Mina, watch them for a moment. I'm going to go see what new tricks I can do."

Confusion colored Mina's face. "Shouldn't we go back to the Outlands now and save our people? They have been long-ing for home all these years."

Gareth waved her away with a grin. "In a minute. I want to play for a bit." He took a step forward and poofed into a black haze once more.

Her arms thrown up in the air in disbelief, Mina could only watch as Gareth's dragon took to the skies with a screech.

Dathon watched the disbelief on Mina's face. "He's drunk on power," he called out. "You know him better than anyone. He could never resist such shallow pursuits."

Mina's face twitched at his words.

His eyes widened slightly. "Is that the kind of leader you want? Is he the king you want to rule over all this?"

Her gaze dropping, Mina visibly swallowed as the conflict brewed in her head.

Dathon gestured to Soleia who was still sobbing. "Mina, the Fae are people just like us. They will do what they must to survive but they are no more evil than we are. Their offenses against our people were just exaggerations Gareth has painted to turn us against each other—while he goes off and *plays*."

Her eyebrows furrowing deeper, Mina blinked a few times as though processing Dathon's words. Her chest starting to heave, she raised her cloudy gaze back up to meet his.

Dathon merely gave her a helpless shrug. "You know I'm right."

Mina's fists clenched at her sides. Even if Gareth was her brother, Mina didn't seem to be an insensible person. And after a long moment, her eyes finally clearing, she let out a sharp, resigned breath and pulled on the clasp holding Soleia's net closed and the ropes fell to the ground.

Soleia immediately ran to Oermilla. "Oma!" She knelt on the stone path, moving to cradle her grandmother's head in her lap and stroke her hair. "O-Oma...you're going to be okay."

Oermilla's gaze shifted to meet hers and a soft smile formed on her wrinkled face. "Soleia, my child...you came home."

Soleia wiped her tears back but they kept falling. "Yes, of course," she sniffed. "Of course, I came home. I'm so—sorry." Clutching at her grandmother's hand, she prompted, "Is there anything I can do?"

Oermilla let out a soft groan. "Don't look so glum. I am

quite alright, child," she assured, letting Soleia help prop her up. "It takes more than an upstart, spoiled dragon to finish me off."

A giant weight lifted from Soleia's chest and she almost laughed. "Oh, thank the gods," she breathed, sitting back on her heels. "Where is Caelina?"

Oermilla waved her hand weakly toward the square. "Caelina ordered to—evacuate the village," she relayed in halting speech. "They are holding the line near the forest outskirts..."

An explosion echoed from down the valley and Soleia snapped to attention again.

"The riot seems to be heading further away," Dathon supplied, casting a wary glance up to the random winged beast flying past overhead. "Perhaps since the village evacuated, Gareth's dragons are wreaking havoc elsewhere. But we should still at least move your grandmother out of the open." He gestured to the temple behind them.

In Soleia's earlier grief, she hadn't noticed that Mina had cut Dathon free of his binding ropes as well. He stood beside Mina and met her gaze briefly in a silent understanding.

Mina's downcast form was still troubled but it was clear, she wasn't going to fight them anymore.

Soleia pursed her lips. Whatever Mina had done, she shared a special bond with Dathon. And like Soleia with Callan, Dathon would forgive Mina anything. She only hoped that Mina's loyalties to her brother's cause had indeed been overridden by her righteous sense.

As Dathon helped carry Oermilla into the temple, Oermilla

clutched Soleia's arm. "That boy with the medallion...his soul is dark."

Soleia's jaw hardened. "Yes. He is a monster."

Oermilla's swayed in her posture as she sat down, seeming to be momentarily winded. She held on to Soleia's arm for support again or simply to emphasize her words. "I could feel it," she rasped. "He has overdosed on impure magic acquired from a single realm. His powers are tethered to the spheres of protection."

Soleia furrowed her eyebrows. "Oma...the spheres," she began, her face already in pained disbelief. "You knew why the magic was dying. You knew what Helene did."

Oermilla took a deep, slow breath and nodded. "It was a great and terrible secret. Helene's rage was uncontrollable, reckless, but even *I* know she lived the rest of her days regretting what she had done."

Soleia looked up to meet Dathon's gaze for a moment. However, regrettably, that fact alone was unlikely to make him forgive Helene. She faced Oermilla again. "Why didn't Helene just reverse the spell?"

Oermilla tilted her head to one side pointedly. "What do you think killed her in the end?"

Soleia's gasp hitched in her throat.

"I once thought there might have been a way to disperse the spheres safely instead but it may be too late. The spheres have been feeding on the magic of the land for decades and have taken on a life of their own. It has grown too strong."

Soleia's eyes narrowed. *Feeding on the magic of the land...* But before she could fully form a hunch in her mind, Oermilla lurched forward in pain with a sharp groan and Soleia jumped to support her back. "Oma, we need to get you somewhere safe, find a healer."

Oermilla let out another soft moan. "I am sorry for hiding so much from you, my child. Caelina was convinced it was for the best." She caught Soleia's arm again. "But I see now, we have all made mistakes—even the ones of us who we think never seem to make any."

Soleia took a deep breath in amused understanding. The statement applied to both sets of sisters—Oermilla and Helene and Caelina and Soleia.

"I think I will just have a little rest here for a moment."

With a small smile, Soleia patted her grandmother's hand and let her lie back down.

Bright flashing light flickering from the sky made Soleia wince and she shot to her feet.

Mina had run back out to the square, already looking up. "What's going on? Is that Gareth?"

"What the hell is he doing?" Dathon stalked over.

Catching up to them in time to see several round orifices appear in the sky, halos of bluish-white spiraling light, Soleia's eyes widened in dread. "A-Are those portals?"

More dragons darted out from each portal, the ferocious, winged beasts cutting across the sky with their loud screeching.

Soleia swallowed hard. "Oh god, if Gareth is calling on all the dragons from the nest to invade this realm, then we are all done for."

Dathon's keen eyesight was studying the influx of creatures in the sky. His face sobering, he shook his head. "Gareth has the home dragons prepared for war." He shot Mina a newly indignant look. "Is this what he has been doing all these years? Is this what you wanted to see? Did you want to be part of this massacre? Did you, Mina?"

"Gareth was only doing it to defend our people!" Mina exclaimed.

Dathon threw up his hands. "This was all Gareth's fault to begin with for angering the High Fae! You already know, if he becomes ruler of all this, there will never be peace."

"I didn't know it would turn out like this," Mina insisted. "We need to do something."

His chin set in determination, he charged, "Mina, you must fly to the outskirts and see if you can find any of our people who are still loyal to me. If Gareth wants a fight, he's going to get a good one."

Mina nodded and without even a second look back disappeared into a bright cloudy haze and a mighty gust of wind as her white dragon took to the skies, blending into the early streaks of daylight.

Helpless, Soleia could do nothing but watch Gareth summon portal after portal, dragon after dragon. "They're going to wreck everything."

Dathon's eyebrows were still furrowed in deep thought. "There must be a way to beat Gareth. He has adopted too many magic amplifiers."

Soleia's heart thumped in her chest as the notion struck her. "The spheres," she breathed. "Oma said Gareth has overdosed on impure energy because the realms are divided. What if someone can bring at least one of the spheres down? Maybe some of the pure, flowing magic will weaken Gareth again."

He narrowed his eyes. "Someone...?"

Soleia pursed her lips. Suddenly, everything was clear. This was her task. This was her strength.

Dathon's eyes widened. "What?"

"You said I was the key," she implored. "The spheres of protection are a form of portal energy, and I can't seem to escape the fact that I'm the only portal summoner around here." She shrugged. "I have to try. It's the only way."

Dathon's tone was grave. He had heard everything Oermilla had said too. "When I said that I didn't know you would have to risk your life. Oermilla said Helene died trying to bring the spheres down."

Soleia rationalized, "She also said there might be a way to simply disperse the spheres instead of taking them down altogether. Maybe it would have worked but Helene never had a chance to test it."

"You don't know that. I won't allow you to sacrifice yourself," Dathon stated thickly.

Soleia was fully aware of the danger it posed but she had never thought twice about sacrificing anything for the sake of her family. Not before with the giant wraith and not now. "You must. I have to save my people, the realm."

"NO!"

Her face crumpling with indignation, she argued, "This is my choice, not yours—"

Grabbing her arm, he pressed his forehead against hers, his jaw setting hard. He nearly growled his declaration, "I am *not* going to lose you."

Soleia gasped at the wild intensity in his stubborn gold-red eyes. Her heart pounded as she studied his face and an ember of hope sparked in her chest.

With the warmth of his firm grip on her arm spreading through her, coupled with the fear and longing on his face, Soleia wavered.

She had only ever wanted to run away from her life.

Perhaps she could look forward to a different future now.

She took a deep breath and nodded after a moment. "Alright then." She threw up her hands, glancing around. "But we have to do something to stop Gareth."

Dathon lifted his gaze back to the sky. "I can fight him. I fought a giant wraith in this village once. Gareth is just a big snake to me."

Soleia's eyes narrowed as her gaze happened upon the curse beads around his neck. "The curse, Dathon..." She approached him to reach for the necklace.

"What are you doing?"

"I need to take the necklace off and break the curse so you can shift. You are the only one who can defeat him."

Dathon caught her arms. "Wait. Is it safe to break the curse right now?"

Soleia gave him a pointed look. "Well, you cannot fight Gareth like this. You would be no match for him in your human form." She peered at his face, questioning his hesitation. "What?"

He averted his gaze. "Your grandmother had once mentioned too...the curse is a sacred bond that once broken cannot be restored."

At the realization of his concern, Soleia couldn't help a

smile. She leaned up against him. "I think it is safe to say we do not need a necklace to be bonded any longer."

His arm came around her to press her tight against him. "Is that a promise?"

Soleia slid her arms up his chest and around his neck. "You must hurry." She hooked the curse beads underneath her fingertips and lifted the necklace up and off his head and a sharp jolt shot back through her body.

"*Ow—dammit!*"

The surge of energy pulsing from the necklace was so powerful it knocked them both to the ground.

"Soleia!" Dathon hastened over to her.

Grimacing, Soleia rolled to one side on the stone path, clutching at her stomach. "Ohhh... Oma should have told me about the sting."

Dathon's forehead creased with palpable worry. "Are you sure you're okay?" But as he turned her over to clasp her against his chest, he seemed to be stifling his chuckle back.

"How does *that* feel?" He gave her a pointed look as though payback for the many times she had sent him crashing face first to the ground with the binding word.

Soleia shot him a suffering look. "Like maybe I should have watched you fall a few more times first."

He brushed her hair back from her face, his voice almost crooning. "I would gladly fall for you as many times as you want."

Unable to resist the light in his eyes, Soleia couldn't even stay mad at him. "You are so annoying," she rasped with a smile.

The curse beads lay innocently in her hands.

Dathon gently took the necklace and moved to slip it around Soleia's neck. His eyes shining, he bent to kiss her forehead. "My soul, my heart."

Still recovering from the sting, Soleia spoke between short gasps. "Well, hurry up and—shift already so I can see your—awesome dragon before I pass out or something..."

Dathon gave her a flat look but couldn't help his wry disbelief. He blew out a deep breath then straightened up before her. "As you wish."

An ephemeral glow covered Dathon's form and his figure glimmered from sight. For a moment, it was as if he was half there and half not. Then a bright cloudy fog burst in the air, growing larger and larger...until a massive golden-winged creature emerged from the haze.

Shimmery scales and bumps covered every bit of Dathon's dragon's stature. His arms and legs had become fore and hind legs, his tail whipped with a mighty swish right behind him, followed by a rush of wind. He flared out his wings to their full extent with a rough grunt as he tested his feet on unfamiliar ground.

Soleia's jaw dropped as her irises filled with his yellow glow. "You're...beautiful."

The golden dragon huffed in pleasure. The giant creature bent its head with a snort, nudging her side with its snout in a sort of endearing gesture. Soleia thought she could almost see the creature smile but she waved him away. "Now...go and kick his ass for me."

Just then, Mina's white dragon soared back into the village

square and upon her landing, Dathon's dragon turned to growl and hiss at her before he finally whirled with a whoosh of his wings.

With a roar, Dathon's dragon shot up into the sky in a golden glimmer—right away slamming into Gareth's black dragon in mid-air, resounding in even more loud outraged roaring.

Still sitting on the ground, Soleia narrowed her eyes up at the figure emerging from Mina's white haze. "What was that all about?"

Mina gave her a wry look. "He told me to make sure you stay put."

Soleia almost scoffed in bemusement.

Mina's gaze was still to the sky. "I found several home dragons still loyal to Dathon willing to fight back. If I could find more perhaps it will even out the odds somehow." Sliding a brief look over at Soleia, she felt compelled to add, "We are not all mindless, evil monsters from the legends."

Soleia gave her an amenable nod. "I understand."

There was another roar of displeasure as a bright beam split the sky.

Soleia squinted against the light of dawn to see which of the dragons had voiced the complaint.

It was the black dragon throwing a tantrum in mid-air.

With thunderous crackling, all the bluish-white spiraling halos spitting out ferocious dragons dissipated altogether, and the skies cleared.

Soleia blew out a breath in humungous relief. That was enough portals for Gareth. She was going to shout in triumph when a bright orange flare erupted in the sky and her gaze snapped upward once more.

Her jaw dropped again. "What in the hell—?"

Mina's eyes widened. "Gareth has fire."

Soleia's gaze darted left and right to follow where Gareth and Dathon's dragons were fighting.

Protest bubbling up in her chest, she threw up her hands. "What? How does Gareth have fire?" She could already imagine that Dathon might be a bit rusty since he hadn't shifted into his dragon form in fifty years. If it was an unfair fight before, it was worse now.

Mina shrugged. "He's adopted many magic enhancers across the realm throughout the decades. Perhaps your grandmother's power has finally filled his threshold."

The two dragons continued to screech overhead. Their battle was far from finished and Soleia couldn't tell if Dathon was winning. She clenched her teeth.

Dammit. Think.

They couldn't take the chance of Gareth overpowering Dathon. Soleia couldn't just sit there and do nothing.

She pushed to stand on unsteady feet. "Mina," she called. "You have to take me to the spheres. I have to try to take it down."

"What?"

Her heart pounding again, she relayed carefully all over again. "Oma had said Gareth's powers are tethered to the spheres. If I take down even one, it might weaken Gareth and help Dathon."

But Mina's forehead creased. "Didn't the old lady say if

you try to mess with the spheres, it would destroy you as it destroyed your kin?"

Soleia swallowed hard through her lie. "Maybe...but she wasn't entirely sure about that."

"Dathon told me to make sure you stay put."

Soleia pressed her lips in a thin line. "Are you willing to risk Dathon's life? Your people need him, don't they?" she prompted. "Besides, Dathon said if I had to do this as a last resort...that it would be fine." She waved in dismissal.

Still highly dubious, Mina narrowed her eyes. "Are you sure?"

Keeping her tone neutral, Soleia watched Mina's face. "Uh-huh."

Mina blew out an exasperated breath. "Fine, I'll fly you to the border but you're going back in your net. I'm not having you ride me and scuff my scales."

Soleia held back her chuckle of relief. "Deal."

This time, as Mina soared through the sky over the valley, Soleia couldn't help her jaw dropping in wonder. Even with the hindrance of a net, Soleia could see the beautiful land-scape of the protected realms of the far north and the majestic mountain range that the rogue dragons had not yet reached.

And unlike before when she had felt trapped, the crisp morning wind blew around her, lightening the weight on her chest, and filling her with great exhilaration.

Despite the recklessness of her plan, she wasn't feeling an overwhelming impending sense of doom.

She had no weapons. She didn't carry any dragon blood.

But the spheres of protection were a runaway cascade of

the most powerful kind of portal energy absorbing all the magic from the land.

Her magic was already here.

And all she needed to do was turn it off. Make the magic gone.

Mina landed in the middle of an empty field and set her down. With a cloudy poof, the dragon shifted back into a person, Mina's eyebrow already quirked in doubt as she studied Soleia's countenance. "Are you really sure about this?"

She waved Mina back. "You'd better go back to the village. I don't know what's going to happen when I try this and I know Dathon would want you safe."

Mina's eyebrow rose again at her notion but she compromised with a nod. "I'll keep a safe distance but Dathon said I needed to keep an eye on you."

Soleia shrugged. "Fair enough."

Mina caught her arm. "Wait." She studied the determined look on her face once more. "I know that face," she told her. "I get that face sometimes. You already know there's a chance you're not going to come back from this, don't you?"

Soleia didn't respond.

Mina cast her a dull look and blew out a huff of disbelief. "Well...I thought I would enjoy watching you die, Fae," she admitted. "But this death of yours will be so very boring."

Tamping down her mirth, Soleia shook her head. "I'm sorry it doesn't live up to your expectations."

Mina pursed her lips, letting her go, but she met her gaze evenly with a small nod. "It is...a very honorable sacrifice."

She couldn't help a small smile and as she watched Mina

walk away, for the first time, she considered that perhaps if things had gone differently, they could have even been friends.

Soleia stepped closer to the magical boundary, looking up to the full height and eyeing it in suspicion before she tentatively raised her hand to press against it.

Her fingers nudged something that was definitely there. It rippled when she grazed it like a pebble tossed into the surface of a still lake before settling again into clear nothingness.

She took a deep breath and closed her eyes.

Prickling ran up her arm as she tried to grab hold of the invisible element, it was a substantial force that resisted, slipping between her fingers, the tighter she tried to hold on to it, the heavier it felt. She tried to close her fist and a jolt shot up her arm straight to her chest.

She collapsed to her knees, already panting.

After another moment, the barrier was tangible in her hands. She squeezed her eyes shut, willing her thoughts to flow through it and its power surged within her. She swallowed hard as she could feel the tenuous shred of magic linking the Fae lands realm sphere to the other spheres across Arcadia.

The wind whirled around her form. The grass and leaves whipped about the empty field. Soleia's hair was in her face as beads of sweat dripped from her forehead. "Aaahh—"

A burst of pain exploded like fire burning her from the inside out and she almost relinquished control to the burgeoning magic forcing its way through her. But she clenched her teeth in strain.

No. Soleia pushed on with an obstinate determination. *You are not weak. You* can *do this.*

The tenuous threads thickened in her fingers and suddenly, Soleia could feel all the spheres contained in one powerful spell. Her chest felt like it was about to bust open at the fullness, the immense force of containing the weight of everything across the land.

With the eyes of her mind, somehow she could see the entirety of Arcadia, the Fae lands, the desert ridge, the market at Cavell, the human settlements, the mountains, and the seas, all at once.

It was as though she was everywhere, was everything.

She quirked her head when a hazy vision crossed her mind —the figure of a tall, young woman obscured by a misty skyline. She had long brown hair and blue eyes and Soleia could see the similarities were indeed striking.

Great-aunt Helene's evanescent form was reaching down toward their devastated village as brilliant sparks of energy rose from the temple in the square...where Oermilla lay.

Understanding hit Soleia's heart like an aching hole gouged within it. And even with all her bravado, Oermilla must have known she was dying as well.

She was joining her sister in the mystical ether.

Soleia cried out loud in her anguish, the emotion swelling in her chest feeding into her magic, but at the same moment, a new, significant infusion of energy bolstered her own. It was tender, soothing, smiling—it felt like...

Family.

Letting her tears fall freely, Soleia focused her renewed

strength on the spheres of protection in her grasp, flinching as she tried to push all the energy out, to disperse it as Oermilla had suggested, and groaning even louder at the effort.

Except Soleia couldn't seem to focus on a single barrier. The spheres would not split apart and the spheres would not disperse. They remained as one giant, connected, heavy cloak upon the land.

Shit.

Soleia bit her lip in knowing dread. She had been clinging to the smallest hope that whatever happened, she could work a way around it, but it appeared there was to be no halfway with her attempt. She was going to have to take down *all* the spheres of protection and suffer the same fate as Helene.

Perhaps she would be seeing her grandmother and Great-aunt much sooner than she thought after all, and this time, not just as apparitions.

She twitched in her vacillation but then shook it off, setting her jaw in resolution once more.

She needed to help Dathon, restore Ipera, heal the land. This was something she needed to do. A sacrifice only she could make, to save the people she loved.

Perhaps this was her true purpose.

Dathon's glimmery wings flew past her reverie and her heart thundered in her chest. He moaned in pain as Gareth struck but he quickly retaliated.

Dathon's dragon twisted away, his tail whipping around in his defense as he shot across the sky before spreading his golden wings.

He was glorious.

Soleia could hear their thoughts as they fought in mid-air.

Gareth scoffed. "You fight dirty now, do you?"

Dathon's response was undaunted. "Just as dirty as you."

Soleia could almost feel his conviction, his spirit, his heart beating with hers. She felt a smile on her face.

Perhaps she would meet him again in another world.

Perhaps this was the freedom she had been longing for after all.

She wasn't scared.

She didn't want to run away any longer.

She needed to do her duty.

To surrender to the magic.

Hoping Mina had kept her word and stayed a safe distance away, Soleia swallowed hard past the considerable lump in her throat, then with the loudest cry of strain, she jerked the hand tangled within the fabric of the spheres down in one violent pull.

* * *

22

Two Souls

When Soleia opened her eyes, she almost balked.

"What the—?" she mumbled.

Her head turned to one side on her pillow, she could see through the gap in the sliding door across the way where Dathon was bowed before Caelina's impeccably regal form as she stood in the receiving room right outside.

Soleia cringed. Was this the afterlife?

Her eyes darted around the familiar room, the woven rug on the tatami, the low table with her pile of books, the wardrobe that spilled clothing right onto the floor, the overpowering smell of Caelina's annoying incense all the way from the next room mixed with the aroma of...chicken soup. It certainly seemed like she was simply back in her room at home in Ipera.

Soleia took a deep breath, satisfied she was actually breathing, and narrowed her eyes.

Okay, so she *wasn't* dead.

She wiggled her fingers and toes under her blanket.

–or maimed.

"That surly girl dragon brought you back unconscious."

The male voice that spoke too close by made Soleia jump and she spun around to see Tobias crouched by the other side of her bed. His one arm was in a sling and there was bruising on his face, injuries from the morning's scuffle.

Donning a few facial nicks herself, Anelis was sitting beside him. She moved to reach over to dig into the bag of dried fruit and nuts Tobias was holding with his good hand before she remarked, "We thought you were dead."

Soleia frowned in puzzlement. "But I'm not."

"Well, we actually thought you had died when the wraith attacked the village last week," Anelis corrected. "We didn't even know you were back. Tobias and I were holding the eastern borders with Stellan and some other mages this morning when we saw the huge flickering lights."

"Caelina was *this* close to cursing everyone so she could leave her protective circle here to assist with the magical wards outside the village but then the fighting suddenly stopped and the dragons all flew away." Tobias scratched his head. "Tell you the truth, we don't really know what happened either. But this afternoon, someone claimed they saw some hunters cross the eastern mountain pass. That's never happened before."

Soleia took a deep breath at the surge of relief coming over her.

Her reckless attempt had worked.

She lifted her hand to touch the curse beads still around her neck and a tremor of energy pulsed through her.

The beads...

She couldn't put her finger on it but she knew somehow the beads had saved her life. Her first instinct was to get up and ask Oermilla. Her heart ached at the recognition that she would never hear her grandmother's wisdom again—whether solicited or otherwise. But she took comfort in the fact that perhaps at least, in the end, she had made Oermilla proud.

Soleia had brought down the spheres of protection.

Arcadia was finally freed.

Then she rubbed her forehead. "Ah dammit, I need to get my horse back."

Munching through his words, Tobias gestured toward what was going on outside the doorway. "Some kind of battle of wills going on out there. That demon's testing your sister's patience."

"He's what?"

"Oh, right, he's not a demon. He's a dragon too, right? A shiny gold one," Tobias spoke up. "We saw him land on the courtyard and change back into human form. That was pretty hot."

Soleia gave his dreamy expression a skeptical look.

Anelis couldn't help a quip, "Doesn't look like your sister approves of your new boyfriend."

Soleia almost laughed. "Look, the day Caelina approves of anything I do—seriously, ow—" She clutched at her stomach at the slight pain as she pushed to sit up in bed.

The door slid open fully and Caelina walked in followed by Dathon.

Caelina's face was already twisted in disapproval. Amused, Soleia watched her sister's nose twitch. She was obviously tamping down something Soleia could only guess was a loud, extensive, and long-overdue telling-off.

Soleia beamed up at her. "Hey, Caelina, how's the baby?" Then she gestured to the forbidding form standing by her side. "You remember Dathon, the evil demon."

Caelina gave Soleia's candor a flat, narrow-eyed look. Her hand cupped protectively over her belly that was beginning to show, she cast a glance at Tobias and Anelis as though to ensure that they too understood that the situation was not to be taken lightly.

Her sister looked perfectly formal but Soleia noted the weary shadow shrouding Caelina's aura. The dark circles under her eyes matched her all-black ceremonial clothes, traditional to wear while mourning. The loss of Oermilla possibly weighed on her more than Soleia could imagine. That plus the strain of carrying precious new life, Caelina seemed...older somehow and even more distant.

It was strange that Soleia had been gone but days and yet it felt like weeks.

"There will be a memorial for Oma this evening, among other things. We lost many good people today," Caelina began, her voice hollow. "There is much to do to clean up the mess the evil ones have brought down upon our realm."

Soleia's heart dropped to her stomach. She was of half a mind to correct that not all of the dragons were evil, present company included, but given the destruction that had rained upon their little village in the early hours of the morning, she decided it would be better mentioned next time.

Caelina was going on, "Suffice it to say, your engagement to Juric is being...reconsidered. His family was displeased, quite a bit alarmed, and rightfully so when you disappeared from the demonstration. No one was certain what had become of you. But given the circumstances, I think they could be made to understand."

She gave the room another general regal look. She seemed hesitant to say any more with her larger-than-intended audience or she could have been genuinely concerned with Soleia's well-being. "We will discuss this more later when you are fully recovered," she declared before she turned on her heel to walk away.

"But I'm—" Soleia wanted to tell her she was feeling fine, better than fine even, but Caelina had already gone.

Dathon hadn't spoken since he'd come in. His gaze was pinned on Soleia alone.

Reading the tension in the room correctly, Anelis cleared her throat and nudged Tobias to get up. "Um...I guess we'll leave you two alone."

Tobias's forehead creased in protest. "Oh—okay, fine." He moved to go but not without turning back once more. "Loved your wings," he gushed to Dathon even as Anelis pushed him out the door.

Once the door slid shut, Dathon sat on the side of Soleia's bed.

There was an edge to his demeanor, his posture tight as though he was also holding something back, or possibly he had too many things he wanted to say and couldn't decide where to begin.

Soleia peered at his face. "How are you?"

Dathon tilted his head as if in disbelief of her asking that question instead of the other way around. "Mina told me what you did."

She wrinkled her nose. "Oh."

"If it pleases you to know, your instinct was right," Dathon started. "Once the spheres of protection were brought down and the pure magic began to flow once more, the impure magic Gareth had collected consumed him. And when he was weakened I was able to..." he trailed off, his forehead creasing in disquiet.

But Soleia understood. Even as Dathon knew he'd had no choice, no doubt the news of having slain your own blood was not something that could be readily shared with ease.

"And Mina?"

A small crack of a smile came to Dathon's face. "Mina has gone back with my people. We are finally able to go home. You risked your life to save my kind. And...for that, I cannot thank you enough—"

"It was the only thing I could think of to do—"

And Dathon finally burst out. "You almost got yourself killed! What the hell were you thinking?"

Taken aback, indignation rose in her chest. "What? Gareth had fire! I was—!" *trying to save you...* She stopped short with a huff, looking away. "Fine, I'll let him have you next time."

Burying his face in his hands, his words were muffled for a moment. "Well, if you keep insisting on recklessly saving my life then I might ask you to put that in our vows."

Soleia blinked. "Our what?"

"Take this."

By the time she figured out what he was doing, Dathon

had slipped a thick metal band with an exquisite family crest onto her index finger and her eyes widened.

"It will keep you safe."

"Keep me safe?" Looking down at the ornately embellished ring on her finger, her cheeks warmed with pleasure. "Is that all?" She looked up to meet his gaze again in skepticism.

Hiding his grin, he tipped her chin toward him, his words a low rumble. "Say yes to me."

She stared up into his gold-red eyes, her elation giving her face a radiant glow. She felt so full that she almost thought she would burst. "Of course."

His own chest swelling, he couldn't help an exultant smile. "I have made arrangements. I am expected back soon to reconnect with all my people, restore order, and ensure the transition goes well. I'd like you to journey home with me."

"To the nest?"

He flinched a little at the term. "There is no nest. Just my home." His expression shifted into another soft smile. "I cannot wait for you to see it."

She beamed at him. "I am certain I will love it."

Dathon lifted her hand to kiss the back of it, the certainty in his eyes wavering for a moment. "I almost thought I lost you."

Her eyebrows furrowing, she looked up to meet his gaze again. "I'm not entirely sure I understand how I survived the fall of the spheres. I could feel them—the power, it ran in me, through me." She shivered at the recollection. "I wasn't strong enough. The spheres wanted to take over and the only way to retract them was to absorb them, *be* them. When the spheres collapsed, I thought I would dissolve into the ether at the same time."

Dathon reached up to finger the smooth beads around her neck. "Dragon souls are more potent than dragon blood. Your soul holds mine. Perhaps when you accepted me on the desert ridge, my soul held yours back, protecting it from fading away."

"A bond stronger than the spheres?"

He leaned his forehead against hers. "Perhaps."

She pursed her lips, considering his words.

Frowning in concern, Dathon pressed his hand to her chest just beneath her throat. "Soleia, this power inside of you, I feel it."

She put her hand over his, a creeping dread stirring in her stomach.

The spheres of protection, the strongest runaway magic spell on the land, would not be dispersed. And such magnitude of energy could not have just vanished into thin air. There was only one place it could have gone.

Dathon dropped his gaze. "I fear a time in the future when I...I may not be strong enough to protect you," he said in an almost inaudible hoarse whisper. He hung his head as though already living the pain.

He was afraid. Afraid to lose her.

Soleia clenched her jaw, reaching out to cradle his cheek to make him meet her determined look. "We can protect each other. You keep saving my life and I'll keep saving yours. When I'm with you, I feel stronger. I feel—more..."

She swallowed hard, almost overwhelmed by what she

wanted to say, what she was on the precipice of feeling. It was more than love.

Their souls were bound.

He was sitting close to her, she could feel his warmth, his ever-calming presence. She had never felt such security around another man before. Dathon was studying the depths of her eyes and she almost drew back at the sudden feeling of vulnerability under his scrutiny.

"Soleia?" he prompted.

She hadn't finished her sentence.

Soleia's chest was already heaving and her heart pounded even harder when his warm hand caressed her cheek. "I feel...I feel whole... With you, Dathon."

Dathon's grip on her face tightened at her confession, and before she knew it, he caught her lips in his in a searing kiss that set her ablaze.

She took his face in her hands and kissed him back just as fiercely as he'd initiated and a hum of pleasure shot throughout her body. Without ceremony, she shifted up on her knees to sit astride him.

He nearly growled, his hands bracing against her hips, clasping her hard against his body and his growing need. His tongue traced hotly against her lips and when she finally parted them, the taste of her made him jerk back, the fire in his eyes meeting hers.

Impatient, Soleia shoved him flat on the bed. He nearly hit his head on the frame and there was an epiphany in his wide eyes, a realization in disbelief as he looked up at her.

"What?" she swallowed, her eyebrows raised.

"I knew it."

"What?"

"You *are* going to kill me, aren't you?"

One corner of her mouth turned up.

"This is what's going to kill me."

Soleia's grin grew mischievous. "Lucky boy." She bent back down to take his mouth in hers.

Dathon's chuckle rumbled in his chest as he folded her up in his arms and rolled them over so his large body covered hers. He pulled away again for a moment to gaze down at her, her blue eyes bright in the daylight streaking through the window.

He brushed a stray lock of messy hair back from her face as if in reverence before a shadow of uncertainty flickered across his face. He raised an eyebrow to prompt, "Are you sure you can handle a dragon?"

Soleia grabbed his head to catch his lips in another demanding kiss, nipping and biting at him.

He groaned in response before murmuring against her mouth, "Make sure you scream my name right. It's Da-thon. Day. Thon. I'm about to make you feel things you've never even dared to conceive you'd ever feel before."

She gave him the same mocking, challenging look. "Promises, promises. Now..." she whispered. "Enough talking."

* * *

23

Epilogue

Callan tugged the hood of his cloak lower over his face.

Passing by the stalls of fragrant spices and chickens for sale, the human patrons of the lively market north of the Semi river traded noisy shouts and milled around minding their own business, not giving him any special notice.

It was as he intended.

Curious, he wanted to investigate the strange new community but Callan couldn't risk being seen and even one of these people letting any of the desert hunters know his whereabouts.

After his betrayal, he could never go back to Cavell.

In some ways, it was a good turn of events. During the two years of working for Therin, Callan had set his primary mission aside, the real reason he had left Ipera to begin with.

News of the spheres of protection coming down was greeted with rejoicing in most corners of the land. Humans and Fae were now free to travel and roam the entire continent of Arcadia once again.

Except it also meant whatever threats had been previously contained in certain realms were now free to terrorize other realms as well.

It was going to provide good, steady employment for talented Fae like him since unprotected villages would be seeking the services of either a mage or a warrior to take care of such threats.

And with the news of the confirmed existence of dragons also being spread far and wide, there was no lack of reaction from the people of Arcadia. Some of fear. Some of awe. Still some of confusion. Certain realms had never even heard of dragons before recently. Then again the protected Fae lands had never even seen humans before either.

These were definitely going to be interesting times.

Callan had also heard of the news regarding the Dragon Prince taking his throne in a faraway kingdom. And apparently he had a new bride.

A corner of his mouth turned up as he continued his stride down the busy market.

He hoped Soleia was happy.

And perhaps once he had found what he was looking for, Callan could fulfill his promise to see her again.

* * *

Follow Callan and Mina's story with **Reign of the Dragon Heir** "The Dragons of Arcadia": Book 2.

Want to read Caelina and Stellan's story? Subscribe to S. R. Breaker's mailing list and get **Arranged to the Fae Warrior** for free.

"The Dragons of Arcadia" series is a precursor to "The Curse of the Arcadian Stone." Read this completed series here: books2read.com/namelessfay1-3bysrbreaker

She was solely created to guard a legendary relic. But when a rogue thief from Earth disrupts her dreary world, her job won't be the only thing she loses.

Preview: The Curse of the Arcadian Stone

The wind whistles through the trees. That's all. No other being could stand to live within the realm of the Mystic Lake.

Over three thousand years ago, a supreme mage cast a spell on a clearing in the Southern Forest. For it kept an artifact. A vestige from the very dawn of Arcadia, the fifth world from the Great Star.

The legend is told that whomsoever possesses this item would be granted the power of the gods.

For millennia, such an object of unimaginable power had proved an undeniable temptation to every creature in the land. To obtain. To master. To wield.

Thus for its safekeeping, it was sealed away in the heart of the Mystic Lake, protected by layers of thick ice—the harsh and brittle shards of enchanted frost for over a thousand years forming on and around the cursed Lake, growing thicker still.

Hidden in the Southern Forest. Whispered as a myth.
Sought no longer by mage or man.
A mere echo of a lost age.
Forgotten...
The most powerful relic in all the known worlds.
It remains undisturbed to this day.

Chapter One

I should know.

I yawned for the 4,380[th] time this year and settled back in my seat, nestled within the branches of the trunk of a tree all but a few steps away from said Lake.

I did say no *other* being could stand to exist within the realm of the Mystic Lake.

None, that was, other than me.

My name? I didn't really have a name.

Although, a soldier who passed by eight hundred years ago had called me *"Magenta"*, attributed to the hue of my sheath ensemble and because my long, often unruly hair was the shade of the sky at dusk.

I remembered him well. Poor guy. I had hoped that he wouldn't be like all the others.

That perhaps he would listen to me and give up his pursuit of the relic. But he was greedy all the same. He died like the rest of them who had ever attempted to take the relic from its resting place.

Turn away any being who ever happened upon this place. That was my job. I was the guardian of the relic and the enchanted realm of the Mystic Lake.

In the early days, knights and mages flocked this area seeking to possess the legendary relic, using brute force, daring skills, or great magic. None of them had succeeded. I'd seen multitudes of them die from my spot up on my tree.

Although as previously mentioned, it had been centuries since I'd last encountered any fiends. Not a single soul had even passed through here for the longest time.

It would have been good of course if only it didn't result in this job being so terribly boring. Not to mention requiring absolutely no effort whatsoever.

Some days I honestly even wished some foolish knight would drop by and casually saunter to his death just so I could have some amusement.

I plucked a leaf off a branch, fashioned it into a flute, and played along to the whistling of the streaming wind. I closed my eyes at the calm stillness of the forest.

After a few moments, I yawned again. *Four thousand three hundred and eighty-one*, I mentally kept track.

On the brink of dozing, I heard a faint commotion and sat up, alert, making the tree I was perched on sway a little.

I sprang up and pounced aloft the redwood treetops in the direction of the noise before stopping to look.

The twilight made it difficult to see anything clearly, except to determine that the commotion had come from the village nearby.

Arcain was the only village remotely close to the Southern Forest. It was a very small village with a population consisting of hunters and gamekeepers, a population that only decreased steadily every year.

Accidents had been known to happen around mystical forests, specifically when villagers wandered too far into the realm and were never to be seen again—which, by the way, was no fault of mine. I was very good at my job.

The noise dissipated and I sighed, having seen nothing exciting for a preoccupation. I headed back to my tree, hopping from branch to branch in no real hurry.

I reached up with both hands to grab a branch above me and pulled myself up. Having nothing else to do, as usual, I swung upward to move to a handstand upon the wobbly tree branch.

I bit my lip as the branch stirred with the wind and I furrowed my eyebrows in concentration. I pushed off, landing on my feet in the next tree. Then I hopped into a cartwheel, coming to rest in another handstand position in the following tree before I crept on, walking on my hands along a branch.

I obviously had too much time to spare.

The truth was that I longed to visit the village...longed to go *anywhere* for that matter. But with the little even I knew about it, I knew I was forbidden to leave the Southern Forest. I knew my duty was to this place. And I was assured that my existence depended upon it.

Needless to say, I often thought about life outside the Forest. It was the most I could do with my infinite existence.

What knowledge I had was ingrained within me. Anything more I learned from my limited contact with the world.

But sometimes when I attuned myself to people's thoughts, I sensed fragments of feelings of wistfulness and it settles on me...within me. I was so weary of these woods.

I crossed one arm over the other on the branch as another light breeze swirled through the Forest. When I glanced up to see how far I had yet to go to reach my tree, I didn't notice that the branch I had been perched on was bending beyond its tolerance. And before I could conjure any sort of spell to fix the tree or slow my descent, it was too late.

I plummeted all the way down as the branch split off from the tree trunk.

"Ow!" I squeaked as I tumbled on the wild grass below.

I sputtered my hair out of my face as I sat up with a groan and looked back up at the tree. I'd fallen from very high and I felt it. My rear end felt it.

"Ow," I groaned again as I stood up. I had to get back to the Lake.

I heard a twig snap and whirled around. The sound echoed guiltily throughout the empty Forest.

I narrowed my eyes at the shadows behind the trees. "Who has come?" I posed the standard question in my halt-and-beware voice, only it seemed to lose some effectiveness with me not up in my threatening big tree.

I cast a furtive glance around but only the wind answered me.

Then I spotted movement from my right and I turned sharply. "Who goes there?" I prompted with a menacing snarl.

After a few moments, a lone figure stepped out from behind a tree.

I squinted as he stepped into the faint light. It was...not a man, but not a child...something in between.

The boy was tall, with dark, tousled hair, and he was wearing an unusual set of clothes. He was definitely not a soldier or a knight. His breeches were loose and his blue hooded shirt donned a symbol resembling a large brush stroke with some writing underneath it that surprisingly, made no sense to me.

"What are you doing here?" He was giving me an odd look. "Are you lost?"

I pursed my lips. I really would have come off more credible if I were up in my tree. *Darn my stupid antics.*

"This place is dangerous." He waved me away. "You better get out of here."

I blinked. That was a switch. He was warning *me* away.

When I still didn't reply, he shrugged and turned to head in the direction of the Mystic Lake.

"Halt!" I stepped forward, raising my hand. "You mustn't go any further."

He stopped and looked back at me. "Halt...?"

I bit my tongue. I often forgot that languages evolved and that I had to adjust my manner of speaking.

"I mean," I began again. "You must not go in that direction if you know what's good for you. If you are seeking the village, it is that way." I pointed in the other direction.

He looked up where I was pointing then back at me. "I've just been to the village and trust me, babe, this direction is good for me."

I shot him a look of ridicule. *Babe?* I was over three thousand years old.

He continued to walk toward the Lake.

"Wait!" I went after him. "Please do not go any further. You must believe me. This is for your own safety." I tried to keep up with his long strides.

"Look babe, my safety is my business." His tone seemed firm, resolute.

"As the guardian of this realm, it actually is my business," I declared. "And I am not a...*babe*." I made a face as I said it.

He paused and turned to me. "Oh, you're the guardian," he spoke as if in realization before his expression turned flat. "So?" he quipped and kept walking.

My generous mood faded when I saw that he was not about to cooperate. "Very well." I shrugged, finally spotting my tree and I drifted up to perch onto one of the lower branches as I watched him walk past below.

"If you keep going, you will die," I called down to him. "No living creature can withstand the magical barrier around the Mystic Lake."

He stopped walking.

"Are you here for the relic?" I queried with a casual tone, leaning against the tree trunk.

"If that relic is a broken little rock, then it looks like I am."

I wrinkled my nose in slight. It was a *gemstone*, I wanted to correct but resolved my protest as irrelevant.

He'd started to walk but stopped again upon my next announcement.

"No one who has ever tried to obtain the relic has survived these woods. Trust me. It will do you no good to try to get it."

That made him look up at me, way up above him, and I felt my words sink in. I always did feel better up in my tree. The Forest was my territory.

I gave him a regal smile down my nose.

"What's your name?"

I blinked again, surprised.

"The last person who asked me that died too," I replied

instead of answering. "He tried to reason about how badly he needed the relic. I'm afraid it does no good to explain to me. I can't help you," I relayed. "I can only warn you. Please leave while you can."

He gave me a critical look, studying me from head to toe before his eyes met mine again. "What's your name?" he repeated, his tone gentler.

"Um…" I was about to explain that I didn't really have a name but then reconsidered. "I was called—Magenta."

"Magenta," he echoed, taking in my overall coloring. "Very apt."

I tilted my head, regarding him with the same critical once-over.

"My name is Josh Richards."

I wondered why he had two names but kept my reply nonchalant. "It's nice to meet you, Josh Richards. It would be nicer if you went on your way—away from here." I gestured toward the village again.

He looked me up and down again as though evaluating his situation. After another pause, he shook his head. "I'm sorry Magenta but I can't do that. I'm not…really from around here. And I need the—relic," he tried out the term carefully, "to be able to go back where I'm from…to see my family and friends."

Family. Friends. I furrowed my eyebrows.

"I need it to get home," he amended.

My eyes widened.

"Yes." He nodded, seeing that I understood. "I need it, see? I've heard of your relic thingy and all the incredible things it can do. But I don't want it to rule the world or anything. I just want to go home. Surely, the guardian of the relic can sense that I don't have any evil intentions."

I did. But that was beside the point. "This is not a test. The relic simply must stay in the Lake. I've told you it does no good to explain to me."

His eyebrows snapped together. "Then what good are you?" He turned to go off in a huff, still headed toward the Lake.

"Oh, damn." I sprang from tree to tree, following him. "Look, you've gone too far—"

"You look," he cut me off, not stopping. "You have no idea what I've had to go through just to get here. There's already like ten armies after me. If I don't get the relic and get the hell out of here, they're gonna kill me anyway so would you just—" He froze in mid-stride.

"Oh no." I perked up and leaped off the tree in time to catch him just as his knees buckled.

Chapter Two

He groaned, making a face in pain.

"See, I told you." I knelt to support him. "Nobody can withstand the mystical barrier around the Lake. You'll just get weaker and weaker as you get closer."

He shook his head. "No, I-I have to..."

"You're breaking out in a sweat," I told him as I helped him stand and turned back to walk us both in the other direction.

A loud commotion made our heads snap up to attention.

"Uh-oh," I mumbled. "I don't think that's a good sound."

He shrugged me off, having easily regained his strength once he had left the immediate vicinity of the Lake. "Dammit, what am I gonna do now?" he muttered. "I didn't come all this way for—"

I had drifted back up my tree, looking toward the horizon to make out where the disturbance was coming from this time or possibly where it was headed.

The village had roused and I was guessing that the people looking for him were asking around for his whereabouts. I also guessed that it wouldn't take them a long time to figure out that he'd gone for the relic and would be arriving here soon.

"You!" the boy called up to me.

I winced, startled at his sudden harsh tone.

"Tell me about the relic," he ordered. "How is it protected?"

I shrugged but obliged. "The Lake has iced all around. The

object rests within the heart of the Lake. It is encased in ice as well. There is absolutely no way to get to it."

"But it's just ice, isn't it? How hard is it to break an ice barrier down?"

"The ice is enchanted, of course" I answered, matter-of-factly. "It won't be so easy to yield."

"Well, has anyone ever tried digging underneath it or jumping into it from above? I mean, it's not like it's iced on top or anything is it?" His expression was intense as though he was in deep thought.

I shot him an exasperated look. "I assure you, everyone has tried everything you may be able to think of. Besides, the protective barrier that you had encountered earlier is set all around the Lake itself, above and below, not just in the ice."

"And—" I couldn't help the mocking in my tone as I went on, as seriously, did he think a strange boy like him, after all this time, could possibly have any new ideas? "Even *if* you somehow got through the barrier and had enough strength to get to the Lake, there's no way you'll last more than a few moments within it. I've already seen soldiers attempt to best the weakening, but they still die all the same once they touch the ice."

He was pacing back and forth on the wild grass beneath the tree. "That's insane. Isn't there some sort of exception? Shouldn't there be a certain chosen person who can overcome the protective barrier?"

"What do you mean?"

He heard the sound of rustling leaves nearing us and looked up in urgency. "The owner," he shot out. "Surely, something as important as this must have an owner."

"The great wizard Aquarius cast the spell to keep the relic sealed. It has no owner," I replied. "No one is chosen. Everyone who gets near it must die."

"That's impossible!" He threw up his hands in exasperation. Then he stopped before his gaze snapped back up to me. "What about you?"

"Me?" I repeated, taken aback.

"Yes!" He nodded. "You've been to the Lake. It permits your presence. The barrier doesn't weaken you."

I tried to follow his hasty logic. "So?"

His eyes shone with anticipation. "Help me."

"What?" I grimaced in skepticism.

"Surely, you must be bored sitting in the same tree all day long, doing nothing except waiting for people to head to their deaths. Help me get the relic," he coaxed. "Then you won't need to stick around here in this boring old forest."

"You must be ill." A haughty laugh fizzled in my throat. "It is my duty to see that the relic does not move from its resting place. I'm not helping anyone, much less you, to get it."

My response was firm—automatic. I had been conditioned to protect the relic. However, my mind had taken a little fancy jaunt and had begun to give his words a second thought.

Get away from the Forest. See the world. Nobody had ever thought to offer me that before in exchange for the relic. Riches and treasures, surely yes. Freedom, never.

The commotion was getting closer and I could already hear the men shouting.

The boy cursed under his breath, watching the direction of the noise in dread.

"Do not worry. You still have time." I maintained a calm

tone. "The Forest will deceive he who does not know it and will lead them around in circles. More so now that it is night-time. And if they try to come too close this way, the barrier will certainly destroy them first."

"There's got to be some kind of way out of this," he mumbled, his stance at a get-ready-to-run.

I pointed north. "Head that way to escape. You should easily lose them in the thick Forest. The barrier does not reach that far."

"Magenta."

His voice had softened a slight and I met his gaze in expectation.

"I'm sorry but...could you possibly lead the way?" he asked, pleading in his eyes. "I'm afraid I'm going to get totally lost if I go on my own."

I started to smile in relief. *He was leaving!* "I am here to guide," I replied dutifully, stepping off my tree and drifting down to the ground beside him.

Unfortunately, three thousand years of immortality had somehow not cured naivety. As soon as I touched down, the boy snatched me up and over his shoulder like a sack.

"Thanks!" he exclaimed and instantly bolted toward the Mystic Lake.

"Hey—!" I protested, struggling against him to make him let me go. No such luck. I looked up even as I thudded against his back and I spotted torches within the Forest.

"Look! Over there!" I heard a shout and the torches moved in our direction.

Uh-oh. I pounded on his back in complaint. "Let me go!

What do you think you are doing? You're going to kill yourself!" I called out my warning.

All of a sudden, I felt something like a jolt within him
as we passed through the invisible protective barrier and his
pace slowed down.

"Go back! You'll die!" I cried out loud. "You'll never survive
this magic!"

But he didn't stop.

I furrowed my eyebrows as I watched several trees whiz by.
We were still getting closer to the Lake. Anybody else would
have fainted dead away at this point, much less a boy of his
age. *How was he still pushing on?*

Then after a few moments, he jumped up to an incredible
height and I felt the cool rush of air from the frozen Lake.

He had reached it! *Impossible!*

I heard a crash from behind me—in front of him—just
before shards of ice went flying all around us.

The boy had broken through the ice around the Lake. And
even still, he was still going.

I screamed aloud when we started to skid on the ice. He
seemed to lose his balance and slid right down the center of
the Lake. I tried to look behind me to see where we were
headed.

Oh no.

We were headed straight for the iced relic dais.

I squeezed my eyes shut as the boy smashed into it with
his feet before we continued to slide across the Lake. Then he
lost hold of me and I toppled back toward the Lake's edge.

"Whoa!" I tumbled onto my side, grimacing even though I
felt little pain.

I shook my hair out of my eyes.

The boy was a few feet away, sprawled out, unconscious.

I looked up as I heard his pursuers charge closer with a loud cry, only for the sound to weaken. They were still unable to surpass the barrier.

I was going to sigh in relief when I looked back again and my eyes widened in horror as I saw the broken dais of the relic in the middle of the Mystic Lake and the hundreds of chunks of ice scattered across the glassy surface.

Oh no! I cursed inwardly. I had managed to screw up my one job in the entire world!

My eyes darted around the debris in search of the cylindrical container of the relic even as I was wondering how long it would take for the Great Aquarius to terminate me once he found out what had happened. But I couldn't spot the relic in all of the wreckage.

I cried out a groan in frustration. I could have blasted this boy to the ends of Arcadia and beyond with an easy spell had I known that he would actually make it this far. I had been trained not to harm humans in the first instance, but in this case, I should have ignored my instincts and been more vigilant. *What a colossal disaster!*

I heard a soft moan and looked up.

He was still alive.

My jaw dropped. "What?" But I had to put my disbelief on hold for the moment. I had to decide whether to drag him out of the Lake or to simply leave him to his fate—which would be certain death against the powerful magic of the Mystic Lake. And I was well aware, the longer I delayed, the more certain the boy's demise.

I huffed. It was his own fault in pursuing the relic. He had to die, I thought, starting to get up. But then I looked back at him again and scowled as I wavered. "Dammit!"

I couldn't just leave him. It was my duty to protect the relic and the Lake *and* the people from it.

I tugged on his arms to sling them over my shoulders so I could carry him out of there. I took a deep breath as I touched off the ice to drift up into a nearby tree.

"Ohh—" I grunted out loud at the effort to drag him away but had resolved to take him all the way out to the limits of the protective barrier so that he could regain his strength.

I hopped from tree to tree even more carefully, headed away from the Mystic Lake, and when he stirred behind me as we left the realm of the protective barrier, I heaved a sigh of relief.

At least I saved a life today, I thought in consolation.

That's when I heard, *"There they are!"*

I whirled around and saw that the men who were after him had gone around the Lake to the other side. They were still hot on his trail—damn, *our* trail!

"Oh no!" I gasped and pounced from tree to tree as quickly as I could even with the heavy burden on my back, heading for the border of the Southern Forest. I waved my hand, summoning a scattered confusion spell so that our pursuers would lose their way in the mischievous Forest.

I was starting to get tired. I didn't normally have this much prolonged physical strain in my everyday life and being away from the Lake was taking a lot out of me.

I was heaving when I touched down on the grass below a big tree at the end of the Forest. And even as I put him down as gently as I could, he still fell partway to the ground as I weakened.

I collapsed against the tree, hoping some of its energy would revive me.

I glanced over at the boy, all in an awkward heap on the ground, then I heaved a huge sigh and closed my eyes.

* * *

Enjoyed the preview?

Read the completed The Curse of the Arcadian Stone: Nameless Fay series now!

Don't miss an epic ending!

S. R. BREAKER is a USA Today Bestselling Author of non-stop action adventure, offbeat YA/NA fantasy romance books. She lives in New Zealand with her husband and two kids.

Suburban mum by day and author by night, she loves to live vicariously through her characters. They don't have to vacuum all day long and are almost always guaranteed to survive any fantastical or thrilling incidents, no matter how treacherous she writes them.

She likes binge-watching TV shows and reading books that take her to far enough unknown worlds—but then still have enough time to wash the dishes after.

Subscribe to her mailing list now for bookish news and get a FREE e-book!

https://subscribe.breakerworlds.com/fantasy

Jump into a fast-paced portal fantasy sci-fi adventure across the multiverse with S. Breaker's completed series **Selfless**.

"They're after you. But which you...?"

Mistaken for her imperiled, notorious genius alternate self, Laney's accidental trip to a parallel world could very quickly turn very deadly.

Read on for a sneak peek...

Sneak Peek: The Selfless Series

They're after you. But which you...? Mistaken identities. Parallel worlds. Government conspiracies. Out of time. Save the multiverse. Save yourself. Don't get erased. Ready?

* * *

"Did we lose them yet?" Laney rubbed her hands over her arms in the freezing cold.

Noah looked intently at the gadget on his arm, tapping a few keys seemingly in mid-air. "I wouldn't count on it."

The rain had abated but it was still dark. It seemed like they had run deeper into the city. She still didn't know where the hell they were.

The whole city was deserted. Old-fashioned cars were stopped in the middle of the streets, some having crashed onto other cars, or onto building facades with faded, cracked brickwork, fallen tarnished bicycles dotted the road, a vaguely iconic-looking red double-decker bus lay on its side at the far end of the street, almost out of view. There was no trace of any other people around, not even animals. Several doors to apartment buildings across the street had been left wide open. It was as though everyone had dropped everything to leave in a hurry.

"What...happened here?" she wanted to know, half-dreading the answer to her question.

"This is the dead city. Ground zero."

"Ground zero. For what?"

He sighed then as if it was no big deal, he relayed, "The global cascade bomb that nearly obliterated all organic life on our world sixty-seven years ago."

"Th-the *what*?" Laney gasped in shock, horrified.

He shot her a slightly annoyed look. "Look, can you keep up? We've already missed the rendezvous window and we're nowhere near where we need to be.

Laney braced her hands on her knees, still trying to catch her breath, and shot him an annoyed look right back. "Hey, we've been running all night. I don't know about the Laney from your world but *this* one is not a triathlon champion."

He didn't respond to her statement. "Come on." He motioned, leading them through a gap in the broken wire fence surrounding a construction site.

"You didn't answer my question earlier," Laney spoke up. "That guy, the one who tried to kill me the other night. He was looking for something. What is it anyway?"

Noah shot her a look, hesitating. "Do you know what spacetime is?"

"Of course," Laney replied dismissively.

He narrowed his eyes at her, dubious.

She blinked again. "I mean," she began. "I know it's like a *science* thing."

"Spacetime is the fabric of the multiverse within which all

our worlds exist," he stated as if he was talking to a child. "Do you know what a wormhole is?"

She pursed her lips.

"What do you learn in school?" he asked in disbelief.

She made another face. "Once again," she said, gesturing to herself from top to bottom. "Normal person. *Not* genius nerd."

Noah rolled his eyes. "Look, the main thing is, there's a device. It makes it possible for a person to move back and forth between two distinct realities."

"Okay."

Noah blinked hard. "No. *Not okay.* What they're ignoring is the probability that this device is going to cause a break in the spacetime continuum, effectively erasing us all from existence. And life as we know it will be over. *Everywhere.*"

Laney mused, "I still don't understand what any of this has to do with me."

"Well, obviously, the government bureaucracies in my world really want this device back—badly. And unfortunately, they think *you* have it."

She stifled an incredulous laugh. "Why the heck would they think *that*?"

"Because...you created it, Laney."

* * *

Enjoyed the preview?

The Selfless Series is a completed series you can read right now!